TO

Happy
B-Day

Have a great

day!!!

Love,
Kendal

VOLUME II
BOOKS 5-8

Pony Pals

Jeanne Betancourt

SCHOLASTIC INC.

New York Toronto London Auckland Sydney
Mexico City New Delhi Hong Kong Buenos Aires

Pony Pals #5: Pony to the Rescue, ISBN 0-590-25244-5,
Text copyright © 1995 by Jeanne Betancourt.
Illustrations copyright © 1995 by Scholastic Inc.

Pony Pals #6: Too Many Ponies, ISBN 0-590-25245-3,
Text copyright © 1995 by Jeanne Betancourt.
Illustrations copyright © 1995 by Scholastic Inc.

Pony Pals #7: Runaway Pony, ISBN 0-590-54338-5,
Text copyright © 1995 by Jeanne Betancourt.
Illustrations copyright © 1995 by Scholastic Inc.

Pony Pals #8: Good-bye Pony, ISBN 0-590-54339-3,
Text copyright © 1995 by Jeanne Betancourt.
Illustrations copyright © 1995 by Scholastic Inc.

12 11 10 9 8 7 6 5 4 3 2 1   4 5 6 7 8 9/0

Printed in the U.S.A.   23

This edition created exclusively for Barnes & Noble, Inc.

2004 Barnes & Noble Books

ISBN 0-7607-5823-9

First compilation printing, June 2004

Contents

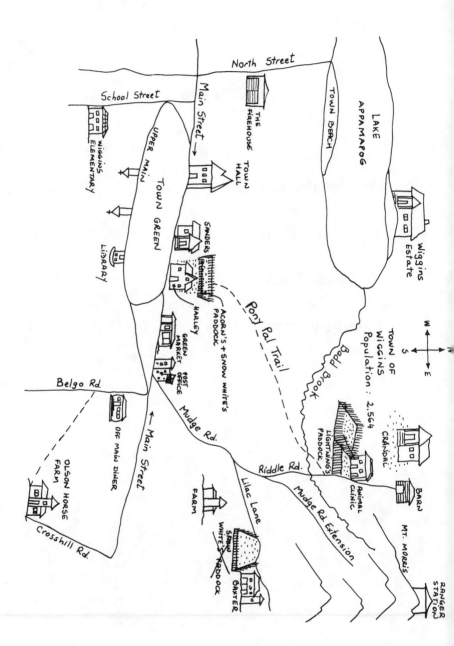

Pony to the Rescue

For my sister, Teri

The author thanks Gay Rickenbacker of Cornerstone Academy and Elvia Gignoux for applying their knowledge of horses to this story.

Contents

Pony Rides

Anna Harley braided blue ribbons into her pony's black mane. As she worked on Acorn, Anna thought about the day ahead and the annual firehouse fair. She loved the fair the volunteer firemen put on for the people of Wiggins. Every summer Anna went to the fair to play games like ring toss and hit the bottle, eat treats like cotton candy and popcorn, and go on rides like bumper cars and the Ferris wheel.

Anna's father was the volunteer fireman in charge of games and rides. This year her father asked Anna and her friends — Lulu Sanders and Pam Crandal — if they would give pony rides at the fair. "Pony rides will be a big hit," he told them. "Kids love pony rides."

The Pony Pals said yes right away. And now the day of the fair was here. Anna couldn't wait for it to begin!

"How does Snow White look?" Lulu asked Anna.

Anna looked over and saw that Lulu had finished braiding ribbons in her pony's white mane.

"She looks beautiful!" Anna said.

"And Acorn looks so handsome," said Lulu.

"My dad is setting up a rope ring for us," Anna said. "And three of the other firemen are going to help us."

"Help us do what?" asked Lulu.

"They'll walk next to the little kids who are riding," Anna said. "That way we can concentrate on leading the ponies."

"That's a good idea," said Lulu. "There'll

be a lot of kids who've never been on a pony before."

Anna saw Pam Crandal and her pony, Lightning, cantering off Pony Pal Trail. "Here they come," Anna said. Pam lived at the other end of the mile-and-a-half trail that made getting to Anna's house easy.

Pam pulled Lightning up beside the other two ponies. Anna petted Lightning's forehead. "You look great, Lightning!" she said. Pam had braided periwinkle-blue ribbons in Lightning's mane, too. And, like Anna and Lulu, Pam wore her periwinkle-blue vest. They were all wearing the official Pony Pal color for the pony rides.

Anna mounted Acorn and Lulu mounted Snow White. "Let's go to the fair," said Pam.

As the Pony Pals rode up North Street toward the redbrick firehouse, Anna could hear music from the fair rides and the voices of excited children. She even smelled the popcorn and cotton candy.

Lulu pointed ahead. "Look," she said,

"there's already a line of kids waiting for pony rides."

Anna counted five kids in line next to a large painted sign. PONY RIDES $1.00.

When Anna dismounted Acorn, a little girl with straight blonde hair was beside her. "Can I ride that pony? Can I?" she asked.

"Sure," Anna said, "that's what we're here for. His name is Acorn."

The girl rubbed Acorn's neck. "He's so cute," she said. "Acorn, you're the best."

"You'd better go back to the line now," Anna said. "But I'll be sure you get to ride Acorn for your turn."

"Okay," the girl agreed.

"What's your name?" Anna asked.

"Rosalie Lacey," the girl answered as she ran back to her place at the head of the line. "I'm six."

For the next two hours the Pony Pals led their patient ponies around the ring — twice around for each rider.

As Lulu helped a redheaded boy down

PONY RIDES
$1.00

from Snow White, she told Anna, "Snow White and Lightning are having a good time. But I think Acorn loves giving pony rides most of all."

Anna agreed. She was proud of her pony. He was gentle with the children and had the cutest expression on his face when they petted him. Anna looked over to see her next rider. It was Rosalie Lacey — again. Acorn noticed Rosalie, too, and neighed softly.

"Are you back for another ride?" Anna asked.

Rosalie handed Anna a ticket. "My mother gave me five dollars for the fair," Rosalie told Anna. "I spent it all on tickets to ride Acorn."

Anna smiled at Rosalie. "Okay," she said. "Let's ride."

As Anna was leading Acorn and Rosalie around the ring, Rosalie asked, "Where does Acorn live? Do you live on a farm or something?"

"We live on Main Street," Anna said.

"Acorn lives in the yard behind my house."

"What house?" Rosalie asked.

"The white one next to the house with the Sanders Beauty Parlor sign," Anna explained.

"I live on School Street!" Rosalie shouted. "That means we're neighbors, Acorn and me. Friends and neighbors." Even though she was in the saddle, Rosalie leaned over and hugged Acorn around the neck.

"Sit up," Anna warned her. "That's not safe."

"Acorn would never hurt me," Rosalie said. "We're best friends."

"He wouldn't hurt you on purpose," Anna explained. "But accidents can happen. If you're going to be around ponies you have to follow some safety rules."

"Can I come visit Acorn?" Rosalie asked. "Please say yes."

"Sure you can," Anna answered. She smiled at the girl. "After all, you're friends and neighbors."

Acorn's New Friend

Later that afternoon, back at the Harley paddock, the Pony Pals cooled down their ponies with wet sponges. Then they scraped off the excess water with sweat scrapers.

"That Rosalie was the cutest kid," Anna told Lulu and Pam. "She's as crazy about ponies as we are."

"She'll be a rider someday for sure," Lulu said.

"She took five pony rides on Acorn," Anna told her friends.

"Kids love Acorn," Pam said. "Look how

my sister and brother always beg to play with him."

Pam Crandal's father was a veterinarian and her mother taught horseback riding. So Pam and the five-year-old Crandal twins — Jack and Jill — grew up around horses and knew a lot about them.

"When I was Rosalie's age," Lulu remembered, "I fell in love with ponies, too. But I didn't get one until I was ten and moved here."

Lulu Sanders moved to Wiggins to stay with her grandmother while her father was working in the Amazon jungle. Now Mr. Sanders was also living at Grandmother Sanders'. Anna knew it made Lulu happy to be with her father again. Lulu's mother died when she was little, so she was especially close to her dad.

"I've had my own pony for as long as I can remember," Pam said.

"She even had one when we were in kindergarten," Anna told Lulu.

"I always gave you turns riding, didn't I?" Pam asked Anna.

"All the time," said Anna. "We had so much fun."

Anna gave her tired pony a handful of oats. "You were terrific today, Acorn," she said. "Thanks."

The next morning, after breakfast and chores, Anna and Lulu saddled up their ponies for a day of trail riding.

Anna heard a girl's voice calling "Acorn! Acorn!" She looked up to see Rosalie Lacey running across the paddock. Rosalie went up to Acorn and gave him a big hug around the neck. Acorn recognized Rosalie and whinnied happily.

"I missed you, too," Rosalie said.

"I guess you found my house," Anna said. She hadn't expected Rosalie to visit so soon.

"Acorn has lived on Main Street all the time and I didn't even know," Rosalie said excitedly.

"Acorn's only been here for a year," Anna told Rosalie. "I got him when I was nine."

"I want a pony, too," Rosalie said. "My mommy won't get me one. She said they're a lot of money. She said we can't even buy a car, why should we have a pony. I told her I liked ponies better than cars."

"Having a pony is a big responsibility," Anna told Rosalie, "and a lot of work."

"I don't care," Rosalie said. She dug her hand into her jean's pocket and pulled out a fistful of coins. "I want another ride on Acorn," she said. "I got money from my piggy bank. See?"

"Pony rides were only for yesterday," Anna told Rosalie.

"We're leaving now anyway," Lulu added. "For a trail ride."

"Can I come?" Rosalie asked. "My mom will let me. All I do all day is go to dumb day camp."

Lulu and Anna exchanged a look. Rosalie was cute, but there was no way they were going to include her on their trail ride.

"We're all experienced riders," Lulu explained. "And besides there are only three ponies."

"I could sit on Acorn with you," Rosalie said to Anna. "I won't wiggle or anything."

"Two in a saddle isn't safe," Anna told her.

Anna checked her saddlebag to be sure she'd packed water with her lunch. Then she swung herself up on Acorn's back.

"We could take turns on Acorn," Rosalie said. "And you can have the most turns. Cross my heart."

Anna shook her head no.

"Pam and Lightning are waiting for us on the trail," Lulu told Rosalie. "We have to go."

"I'll bet you'll do something special today at day camp," Anna said. "Something that's loads of fun."

"I want to play with Acorn today," Rosalie said sadly.

Lulu and Snow White were already going through the open paddock gate.

13

Rosalie walked alongside Acorn and Anna. "Please let me come," she whined, "please . . ."

Anna moved Acorn into a trot. Rosalie picked up her pace, too. Why couldn't the girl just go to day camp and leave her alone?

"Don't get so close to a moving horse and rider," she warned Rosalie. "You could get hurt."

Rosalie finally gave up and slowed down. Anna and Acorn passed through the paddock gate onto the trail. Anna signaled Acorn to move into a canter. But Acorn slowed to a walk instead.

"What's wrong, Acorn?" Anna asked. Acorn turned his head. He wanted to go back to the paddock. Anna looked behind her.

Rosalie was standing at the gate, looking sad. Acorn turned his head and neighed at the little girl.

Lulu, who was ahead of Anna and Acorn

on the trail, called to Anna, "What's wrong?"

"You go ahead," Anna called back. "We'll catch up." She turned Acorn around. She didn't have to urge her pony to move now. He trotted straight back to the paddock and up to Rosalie.

"Oh, Acorn," Rosalie said. "You came back."

"He's still going on a trail ride," Anna told Rosalie. "But we'll be home around four o'clock. If your mother says it's okay, come over after day camp. You can help me groom and feed him."

"Yippee!" Rosalie cheered. "Did you hear that, Acorn? I'm going to feed you!"

Rosalie's Surprise

Pam and Lulu were waiting for Anna at the three birch trees that marked the midpoint of Pony Pal Trail.

"We thought Rosalie would be riding Acorn and you'd be running along behind them," Lulu joked.

"That girl is crazy about Acorn," Anna said as she leaned over and patted Acorn on the neck. "I can understand why. Acorn's great."

"Are you and your great pony ready to go trail riding?" Pam asked.

"Let's go," Anna answered. It was her turn to lead. She steered Acorn toward the trail on the Wiggins estate that started behind the birch trees. He responded immediately to her direction. He was still her pony.

First the Pony Pals went to their favorite field on the Wiggins estate and took turns jumping their ponies over a low stone wall. Then the ponies munched on fresh grass while the girls ate their lunch beside Badd Brook.

On the way home they stopped by the paddock at Ms. Wiggins' mansion to say hi to her black horse, Picasso, and her old Shetland pony, Winston.

Ms. Wiggins waved to them from her painting studio. They waved back. They all liked Ms. Wiggins. Especially Anna. Anna and Ms. Wiggins had a lot in common. They were both dyslexic and had trouble learning how to read. And they were both terrific artists.

By four o'clock the three girls were back

on Pony Pal Trail. That's when Pam reminded Lulu and Anna that they were going back to her house for a picnic and barn sleepover.

"Oh, no!" Anna said. "I thought that was tomorrow. I told Rosalie she could help me feed and groom Acorn when I got back."

"Maybe she forgot about it," Pam said.

"Are you kidding?" Anna and Lulu said together.

"You could call your house and have your mother tell her to come back tomorrow," Lulu suggested.

"My mother's not home," Anna said. "She's working at the diner. Besides, Rosalie would be so disappointed." Anna sighed. "I gotta go back."

Anna left her friends and galloped home along Pony Pal Trail.

She wasn't at all surprised to find Rosalie waiting for her and Acorn at the paddock gate. Anna slowed the pony down and halted next to Rosalie.

"I have a big surprise for you," Rosalie told Acorn. "Wait till you see."

"And I have a surprise for you," Anna told Rosalie. "How would you like to ride Acorn back to his shelter?"

"Yippee!" Rosalie shouted. She wanted to hold the reins herself, but Anna knew that it was safer if *she* led the pony. "You can get down by yourself," Anna told her.

Anna saw Rosalie's "surprise" before they reached the shelter. It was three *huge* piles of hay laid out on the shelter floor. Each was topped with a mound of oats and carrots.

"I made supper for the ponies," Rosalie bragged. "Where're the other ones?"

Anna tried to stay calm as she explained to Rosalie that the other two ponies were eating at the Crandals'.

"Can Acorn eat his?" Rosalie asked.

"You never give a horse that much food, Rosalie," Anna scolded. "You only give them the exact amount you want them to eat. Overeating can make horses sick. It can even kill them."

"I'll clean it up," Rosalie said quietly.

"I'll do it," Anna told her.

Anna took off Acorn's bridle and saddle. She let Rosalie help her sponge down Acorn and showed her how to use the sweat scraper. Then Anna turned Acorn out in the paddock.

"Can I play with him?" Rosalie asked.

"Yes," Anna said. "But keep him away from all this food. I don't want him getting into it."

Anna went to the three mounds of food. Her first task was to separate the oats from the hay. Every once in awhile she looked up to check on Acorn and Rosalie. Rosalie was following Acorn all around the paddock. They were having a great time.

Anna wasn't having fun. It was hot in the shelter and the flies were as interested in Anna as Rosalie was interested in Acorn.

Suddenly, Rosalie came running up to

her. Acorn was close behind. That meant Anna would have to keep Acorn from getting into the piles of food — again. "I thought I asked you to keep Acorn away from the shelter," Anna said.

"He follows me everywhere," Rosalie said proudly. "I can't help it. And he wants to give me another ride."

"Oh no he doesn't," Anna said. "He wants to slow down and have a rest."

Acorn nosed around Anna and started munching some oats. "And keep him away from this mess," Anna shouted. "Haven't you caused enough trouble for one day?"

"I'm sorry," Rosalie said softly. "I thought you'd be glad I made the ponies dinner."

Rosalie turned and walked slowly across the paddock. Acorn followed her. Anna watched to be sure Rosalie closed the gate behind her. She didn't want Acorn to follow Rosalie home.

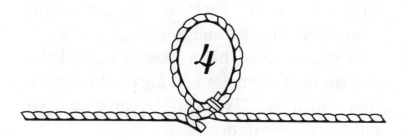

Anna's Great Idea

When Anna got to the Crandals', she let the twins help her unsaddle Acorn. Then she turned him out in the paddock with Lightning and Snow White.

Anna laughed when she saw the dinner that Pam and Lulu had prepared. They'd set out three individual pizzas on their favorite picnic rock near the paddock.

"We made them ourselves," Pam said.

Anna told Pam and Lulu about the three mounds of food Rosalie had prepared for their ponies. "It looked something like this," she said. They all giggled about "Pony Pal Pizzas" and dug in.

Between bites they talked about all the fun things they'd done so far on their summer vacation. "We still haven't camped out," Lulu reminded them.

"We sort of camp out when we have barn sleepovers," Anna said.

"I mean camping out in the wilderness," Lulu said. "With a tent."

"Would we take our ponies?" asked Pam.

"Absolutely," said Lulu. "And enough food for two days."

"Our parents would never let us," Anna said sadly.

"There has to be a way," said Lulu.

They all thought silently for a minute. Between them they knew they'd find a solution to this Pony Pal Problem.

"I've got it," Anna exclaimed. "We could camp out on the Wiggins estate. Our parents know Ms. Wiggins. And she'd know

where we were and everything."

"And our ponies would be rested in the morning," said Lulu. "So we could start from our campsite and go on Wiggins' trails we've never been on before."

Anna and Lulu were ready to hit high fives, but Pam wasn't. "We still have to ask our parents, *and* Ms. Wiggins," she said.

"Let's start with Ms. Wiggins," Anna suggested.

"My dad's having supper with her at the diner tonight," Lulu told the others.

"So let's go to the diner," said Pam.

Anna patted her pizza-filled stomach. "I'm starving," she said with a giggle.

When the three girls walked into Off-Main Diner, a voice called out, "Hey, look who's here." It was Lulu's father. They went over to the booth where he and Ms. Wiggins were eating blueberry pie with ice cream. "Order yourselves dessert on me," Mr. Sanders offered.

"Thanks," they all said together.

Ms. Wiggins told Lulu's dad how the girls and their ponies had visited Picasso and Winston earlier in the day. "Girls," she said, "there are interesting trails over on the west side of the estate. I'd love for you to ride on them sometime."

The Pony Pals exchanged a look. They couldn't believe it. It was as if Ms. Wiggins had read their minds.

"That's why we came looking for you," Lulu said.

"To ask you a favor," Pam put in.

"That has to do with those trails," Anna added.

The girls explained their idea of camping out on the Wiggins estate.

"Then our ponies will be fresh in the morning," Anna said, "and we can explore the trails to the west."

Ms. Wiggins smiled. "I know the perfect campsite for you," she said. "It's near a stream and not too far from my house.

There's a small corral that will be perfect for your ponies. And I have a tent I can set up for you."

Mr. Sanders said Lulu could camp out as long as the campsite was near Ms. Wiggins' mansion. Anna got her mother from the diner kitchen. After talking to Lulu's father and Ms. Wiggins, she agreed that Anna could go on the camping trip. Pam phoned her parents. They agreed that if Ms. Wiggins was involved, Pam could camp out, too.

"Now let's plan the trip and write everything down," Pam said.

The girls ordered brownies and milk and got paper and pencils from the kitchen. Then they went to their favorite booth to eat dessert and prepare for their camping trip.

"We can put our food and clothes in the saddlebags," Anna said.

"And move the sleeping bags to the back of the saddles," said Lulu.

Anna drew a pony outfitted with gear for a camping trip. Pam labeled the drawing.

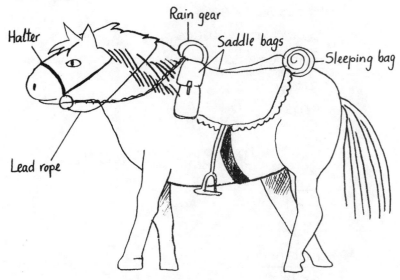

Halter

Rain gear

Saddle bags

Sleeping bag

Lead rope

"Next we should plan our menus," Lulu said. "Then we'll know what food we need to buy."

"This trip is going to be so much fun," said Anna.

The girls decided what they and their ponies would eat on the camping trip. Lulu wrote their menus down.

LUNCH — DAY ONE

For us:

peanut butter and jelly sandwiches

apples

boxed fruit juices

For ponies:

water

grass

SNACK — DAY ONE

For us:

trail mix

water

For ponies:

water

apples

The girls were planning SUPPER — DAY ONE when they heard a familiar voice yelling, "That's them, Mom. The girls with the ponies!"

Oh, no, Anna thought, as she looked up to see Rosalie and her mother at the counter. Her mother's hair was blonde and straight, just like Rosalie's. Rosalie came over to the Pony Pal booth. "Where's Acorn?" she asked.

Anna explained that Acorn and Snow White were having a sleepover with Lightning.

Rosalie looked at the papers spread out over the table. "How come you're doing homework?" she asked. "It's vacation."

"We're going on a camping trip," Lulu explained. "We have to make lists so we don't forget anything."

"We're real busy right now," Pam added.

"Rosalie," her mother called sharply. "Come get this ice-cream cone before it melts all over me."

"Coming," Rosalie answered. "See you tomorrow," she told the Pony Pals.

"Those are my new friends," they all heard Rosalie tell her mother.

Anna sighed and went back to working on the lists. At least Rosalie wouldn't be going on their camping trip.

Beware of Rattlesnakes

The next morning the Pony Pals woke up from their sleepover in the barn. They fed their ponies and talked about the camping trip. They were still talking about their trip while eating breakfast in the Crandal kitchen. "I can't believe we're finally going *camping!*" Anna exclaimed.

After breakfast the girls saddled up their ponies and rode onto Pony Pal Trail. But they weren't going on a long trail ride. They were going straight to the Harley paddock.

The girls wanted their three ponies rested for the big camping trip the next day. Besides they had to shop for groceries and supplies.

They were in the fruit and vegetable section of the Green Market when Anna saw Rosalie's mother. She was weighing grapes for a customer.

"Look," Anna said to her friends, "that's Rosalie's mother."

They brought their bag of apples over to the woman.

"Hi," Anna said.

"Hi," Mrs. Lacey said back. "You're the girls with the horses." She didn't smile when she said it so Anna couldn't tell if she was being friendly or not. "Rosalie won't stop talking about horses," she said. "Day and night that's all I hear."

"I know," Anna said. "She really loves them."

Rosalie's mother sighed as she weighed the apples. "Why can't Rosalie like goldfish?" she asked no one in particular. "Goldfish I could handle. Or even a gerbil." She marked the price of the apples on the bag and handed it to Anna. "Don't encourage her, okay?" she said. "Because there's no way on earth that girl is ever going to have a horse. I have enough trouble paying the rent and buying food and clothes for her and her brother."

"We don't encourage her," Anna told Mrs. Lacey.

Another customer handed Mrs. Lacey a bunch of bananas to be weighed.

" 'Bye, Mrs. Lacey," Pam said.

"Yeah. 'Bye. You all have a nice day," she said. "You and those horses."

Anna didn't bother to tell her that their horses were ponies. And that ponies were smaller than horses. She knew Mrs. Lacey wouldn't care.

The Pony Pals were climbing the back stairs to Anna's house when Anna noticed Rosalie's blonde head bobbing around the paddock. Rosalie was back — again. When

she spotted the Pony Pals, Rosalie ran across the paddock toward the house. The three ponies trotted in a row behind her.

"She's like the Pied Piper of ponies," Lulu giggled.

The three ponies stopped at the fence and watched Rosalie hop over the top. Rosalie ran past the vegetable garden and up the stairs. Anna noticed she had a periwinkle-blue ribbon in her hair. The Pony Pal color!

"Rosalie, does your mother know where you are?" Anna asked.

"My brother does," she answered. "He takes care of me after day camp. He's thirteen. I told him I'm helping you get ready for your camping trip. He said you should watch out for rattlesnakes. He said rattlesnakes like dark, warm places — like sleeping bags."

"Is your brother Mike Lacey?" Pam asked.

"Uh-huh," Rosalie answered. "That's him."

The Pony Pals exchanged a look. They all knew Mike Lacey. He was best friends with the meanest, most annoying boy in the eighth grade — Tommy Rand. Mike Lacey was the *second* meanest, most annoying boy in the eighth grade.

"Tell your brother thanks for the advice," Lulu said. "And tell him we're not afraid of snakes. I camped a lot with my dad in places that had lots of snakes. Even poisonous ones."

"Maybe your brother's the one who's afraid of snakes," Pam added.

Anna thought, Rosalie has a mother who doesn't like horses and a pain for a brother. What about her father?

"Does your dad live with you?" she asked Rosalie.

"Not anymore," Rosalie said. "He lives in Ohio."

For the first time Anna felt sorry for Rosalie. But not for long.

"Can I ride Acorn?" Rosalie asked.

"Not today," Anna answered. "The ponies are resting for the trip."

"Can I have a ride when you come back from the trip?" she asked.

"I suppose," Anna answered.

"Can I have two rides because you'll be gone two days? Please say yes."

"We'll see," Anna answered.

Acorn neighed and Rosalie ran back to the paddock yelling, "Two rides on Acorn. Yippee!"

The next morning the Pony Pals met in the Harley paddock. Anna tied her sleeping bag to the back of her saddle. "This is going to be great," she said. Anna noticed that Rosalie was running across the paddock toward them. Anna was so happy about the camping trip that even Rosalie couldn't spoil her good mood. "Hi, Rosalie," she said cheerfully.

Rosalie didn't seem to hear her. She was hugging Acorn. "I came to say good-bye,

Acorn," she told the pony. "Have fun and come back safe."

Just then Lulu's father came out to the paddock. "Here's a little something for your trip," he said. He handed each of the campers a red plastic whistle. "Use these if you get separated. Or to signal if you need help."

Mrs. Harley was coming across the paddock carrying a package. Anna thought it looked about the size of three big brownies. But the package wasn't brownies. It was a first-aid kit. "I made this up for you," her mother explained. "There's antiseptic, Band-Aids, and an Ace bandage." Anna put the first-aid kit in her saddlebag next to her flashlight.

Grandmother Sanders came out, too. "I just heard on the radio that it is going to be very cold tonight," she said. "Maybe you should wait for better weather."

"We'll be okay, Grandma," Lulu said. She gave her grandmother a hug.

"Can I walk partway with you?" Rosalie asked Anna.

"It's time for you to go to day camp," Anna told her. "We're only going to be gone for two days."

"Oh, all right," Rosalie said. " 'Bye." She gave Acorn one last hug.

S.O.S.

At first the girls were riding on familiar
trails. "So far it's just like a normal day of
trail riding," Pam said.

Once they got to the Wiggins' mansion,
Anna took out the map Ms. Wiggins had
made for them. She checked the map and
pointed with her riding crop to a wooded
area on the right. "The campsite is this direction," she said. "There's the trail."

Anna and Acorn led the way. The campsite was an open area with dry leaves and
pine needles. A gray, dome-shaped tent was

set up on one side of the clearing. On the other side there was a small pony corral closed in by an old wood fence. Through the trees Anna saw the clear sparkling water of a stream.

"Sh-hh," Lulu said. "Listen." Even the ponies stayed perfectly still while they all listened to the gurgling of the stream and the chirping of a lone bird.

"It's perfect," Pam whispered.

The girls dismounted their ponies. Then they undid their sleeping bags and saddlebags and put them on the ground. Next they removed their ponies' tack. They left on bridles and halters so they could lead the ponies to the stream for water and grass.

After they put the ponies in their corral, Anna shouted, "Race you!" The Pony Pals ran across the clearing to the tent.

They all got there at the same time, but took turns crawling through the flap opening.

"It's bigger inside than it looks from the outside," Pam said.

"And look," Anna said, "Ms. Wiggins left us stuff."

In the middle of the tent floor there was a red bucket, a plastic gallon jug of water, and a note.

Pam opened the note. The others looked over her shoulder as she read it aloud.

Dear Campers:

I will come by for dinner. We'll make a campfire. Have a great afternoon trail riding.

Love,
W.

P.S. The bucket is so your ponies can have stream water in the corral tonight. The bottled water is for you.

The girls ate lunch in front of their tent. After lunch Lulu strung their food up in a tree so animals wouldn't get it. Then they put the rest of their supplies in the tent.

Even though Anna didn't believe anything Mike Lacey said about snakes, she decided to leave her sleeping bag rolled up until she went to bed. She noticed that Pam and Lulu did the same thing.

Acorn nuzzled Anna happily when she tacked him up for an afternoon ride. "We're going places we've never been before," she told him. "And then we're coming back here for the night. It'll be very dark and fun." She gave her pony a hug. It was great to have Acorn all to herself again.

The Pony Pals followed the map Ms. Wiggins had made for them of the western section of the Wiggins estate. It was as beautiful and interesting as Ms. Wiggins had promised. They found a pond with a turtle as big as a dinner plate. And when Pam was in the lead position, she saw a fox run across their path.

At the top of a particularly steep hill, they walked their ponies over to the edge of the trail to look at the view. "This is the highest we've ever climbed," said Anna.

"Oh, look!" Lulu said. She pointed to a large hawk gliding on a wind current.

"There's Mount Morris," Pam said, pointing to the east.

"Someday we'll camp over there," said Lulu.

They were going down the steep hill when they heard a high-pitched sound. "Was that a bird?" Pam asked.

They heard the noise again. This time there was one short blast followed by a long one and another short one. "That's the S.O.S. signal my father and I use," Lulu said.

"Someone's in trouble," Anna said.

"Or is trying to find us," Lulu said. "Someone who knows the signal."

Lulu took out her whistle and blew one long whistle. "That's what we do to let the other person know we heard them," she explained.

A long whistle answered Lulu's signal. This time the girls noticed that it came from the direction they'd come from.

"Let's go," Lulu said. "Whoever needs us is coming this way."

"You take the lead," Pam told Anna. "Acorn's best on this rocky terrain. He gives our ponies confidence."

As they went down the steep incline, Anna felt proud of Acorn. But she was also feeling afraid. Who was sending them an S.O.S. signal? And why?

When they reached the foot of the hill, Pam blew her whistle. This time the answering whistle was even closer.

A few minutes later Anna saw Picasso and Ms. Wiggins coming around a bend in the trail. Anna turned in the saddle and told the others, "It's just Ms. Wiggins."

Anna figured Ms. Wiggins was looking for them just to be sure they were okay. But when Ms. Wiggins got closer, Anna saw a grim look on her face. Something was terribly wrong.

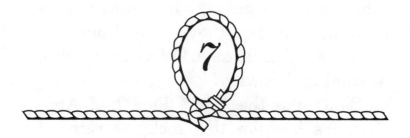

Emergency!

The Pony Pals pulled their ponies up in front of Ms. Wiggins and Picasso.

"What's wrong?" Anna asked.

"Rosalie is missing," Ms. Wiggins answered. "Lulu's father called to tell me. We decided I should find you girls. You might be able to help."

"What could have happened to her?" asked Anna.

"We just saw Rosalie this morning," said Lulu.

"Did someone kidnap her?" asked Pam.

"Let's go back to your campsite," Ms. Wiggins said, "and I'll tell you everything I know."

The three girls and Ms. Wiggins rode in silence. They were all concentrating on keeping up a good pace. And worrying about Rosalie.

While the ponies and Picasso drank from the stream and munched on grass, Ms. Wiggins told the girls what she knew.

"Mike Lacey went to pick up his sister at day camp," she began. "They told him that she hadn't been there all day. He went over to your house, Anna, to see if Rosalie was there. Your mother told him that Rosalie had been by in the morning. And that she said she was going to day camp.

"Next," Ms. Wiggins continued, "Mike went to the Green Market to tell his mother Rosalie was missing. They both checked their apartment to make sure Rosalie hadn't gone home while Mike was looking for her. Then they phoned their friends and neighbors in town. It seems no one has seen

Rosalie since nine o'clock this morning. Mrs. Lacey notified the state police. Everyone is looking for Rosalie. As of an hour ago she hadn't been found."

Pam looked at her watch. "It's five o'clock now. Rosalie's been missing for eight hours."

They were all silent for a few seconds as they thought about what a long time eight hours could be. Anna was trying to figure out where Rosalie went. Had she cut day camp and just forgotten about the time? Or had she wandered off by herself and gotten lost?

Anna looked over and saw that Acorn was watching her. Anna thought he had a sad look in his eyes.

Ms. Wiggins broke the silence. "Mrs. Lacey said Rosalie spent a lot of time with you three over the last few days."

"She kept hanging around us," Anna told Ms. Wiggins. "It started with the pony rides at the firehouse fair."

"She can be a pain," Lulu said. "But we

were nice enough to her. Especially Anna."

Anna wasn't sure she'd been "nice enough" to Rosalie.

"Do you have any idea where Rosalie might have gone?" Ms. Wiggins asked.

The three girls looked at one another and nodded. They all had the same idea.

"Maybe she tried to follow us," Anna said. "She's always wanting to do whatever we do."

Pam and Lulu said they agreed with Anna.

"Maybe we should form our own search party," Lulu said to Ms. Wiggins.

"We could start here and go back over the trails we took this morning," suggested Pam.

"And we should ride our ponies when we're looking for her," said Anna. "That way we can move fast and give Rosalie a ride if we find her. Acorn likes Rosalie and I think he'd want to help."

Ms. Wiggins agreed that the girls should look for Rosalie. Meanwhile, she told them, she'd ride Picasso back to her place to phone the Town Hall. "That's where they've set up headquarters for the search party," she explained. "I'll tell them you think Rosalie might have followed you. I can fax them a map of the trails. Then they can start *their* search from where you started out this morning."

Ms. Wiggins put the bridle on Picasso. "I'll meet up with you on the trail," she said. "If Rosalie's already been found I'll signal by one short and one long blast of my whistle while I'm riding."

"And if we find her we'll do the same," Lulu said. "That way you can let everybody know."

"If you find Rosalie in bad shape, or you need help yourselves, don't forget to send out the S.O.S. signal," Ms. Wiggins said.

"Maybe you should tell the search party the signals we're using," Lulu told Ms. Wiggins.

"Good idea," she said. Ms. Wiggins

mounted Picasso, wished the Pony Pals good luck, and rode off.

Anna looked up at the sky. The blue sky of a few minutes before had turned gray with storm clouds, and the temperature had dropped.

Anna shivered.

"All Rosalie had on this morning was shorts and a T-shirt," Lulu said.

If Rosalie was in the woods, Anna thought, would they be able to find her by nightfall? Or would the six-year-old girl be spending the night alone in the woods without shelter, warm clothes, food, or water?

The Clue in Badd Brook

The Pony Pals got ready for the big search. Anna put her extra sweater in her saddlebag next to the first-aid kit and flashlight. She refilled her water bottle and put that in the other saddlebag with her trail mix.

Lulu got the idea to hang their whistles around their necks. They used the rawhide shoestrings they'd brought for emergency bridle repairs.

The girls worked quickly and efficiently. This wasn't playing. This wasn't a game.

They had an important job to do. Rosalie's safety was at stake. Maybe even her life.

As the Pony Pals put the bridles on their ponies and tightened the saddle girths, they talked about how they would conduct the search.

Lulu knew a lot about tracking animals and people from her many camping trips with her father.

"We're looking for signs that she's been on the trail — or where she might have gone off it," Lulu told Pam and Anna. "So keep an eye out for footprints, broken branches, or pieces of torn clothing."

"What colors was she wearing this morning?" Pam asked.

"She had on a yellow T-shirt," Lulu remembered. "And red shorts."

"And that periwinkle-blue ribbon in her hair," Anna said. "Like the ones we used in our ponies' manes for the firehouse fair."

As they mounted their ponies, Pam said she'd look for clues on the left-hand side of

the trail. Lulu said she'd look on the right. Anna, who took the lead, would watch for clues straight ahead.

They rode in silence so they could concentrate on searching for clues and listening for any sign of Rosalie. But every five minutes or so the Pony Pals purposely made a lot of noise. They hollered out "Rosalie." Then they halted their ponies and listened carefully to hear if Rosalie answered.

"Look how good our ponies are about all the noise we're making," Lulu commented to the others.

"I think they know we're doing something important," Anna said. She leaned over and patted Acorn's neck. "You're going to help us find Rosalie, aren't you, Acorn?" Acorn nickered in response.

As the search continued, Anna wondered how Rosalie felt. Anna knew that if *she* were lost in those woods when she was only six years old, she'd be *terrified*. Anna decided that Rosalie would be thinking all sorts of horrible things — like never being found and starving to death. Maybe she would imagine swarms of killer bees or millions of biting red ants or attacking wolves. And Rosalie definitely would be remembering what her brother said about rattlesnakes.

Soon the Pony Pals came to the wide section of Badd Brook that they'd crossed in the morning. Fast-moving water rushed over boulders and rocks.

"She couldn't cross this without a horse," Lulu said.

"But what if she *tried* to cross it," Anna wondered out loud. "Then fell and got dragged by the water."

"Let's walk along the edge of the brook," Lulu suggested, "toward the waterfall."

This was the first time any of them mentioned the waterfall. And that's all that was said. The thought of Rosalie being swept over the waterfall was too scary to say out loud.

While Acorn stepped carefully along the

uneven bank of the brook, Anna kept a sharp eye out for clues. Suddenly, she noticed something bright blue in the water. She halted Acorn and dismounted.

"Why'd you stop?" Pam asked as she halted behind Anna.

Anna slipped Acorn's reins over his head and handed them to Pam. "Hold him," she said. Then Anna jumped on three rocks to get closer to the flash of blue color in the water. Planting both her feet on the third rock, she squatted and put her hand in the cold stream. She pulled out a ribbon that had been caught on the sharp edge of a mossy rock. Anna jumped the rocks back to solid ground. She held up a periwinkle-blue ribbon for the others to see.

Without saying a word, the other two yelled "Rosalie." They waited and listened carefully. The only answer they heard was the sound of the brook rushing toward the waterfall.

The Pony Pals were on foot leading their ponies toward the waterfall when Acorn suddenly stopped in his tracks. "He doesn't want to go this way," Anna told Pam and Lulu.

"Maybe he's afraid of the sound of the waterfall," said Lulu.

"He's never cared about that before," Anna said.

"Maybe he got a pebble in his hoof," suggested Pam. "If you need the hoof pick, I've got it in my saddlebag."

Anna checked Acorn's hooves. No pebbles. But Acorn still wouldn't go forward.

"What is it, Acorn?" Anna asked her pony. "What's wrong?"

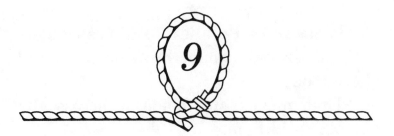

In the Deer Run

Acorn neighed and lowered his head. What if he has colic? Anna thought. She knew that horses could die from colic. But Acorn didn't seem sick. He was just sniffing the ground and pawing at a mess of deer hoofprints in the mud.

Anna bent over and looked more carefully at the ground herself. There, among the deer hoofprints, she saw the clue they'd been looking for. The imprint of a small sneaker.

"Look!" Anna pointed to the ground. Pam and Lulu walked over.

"It has to be Rosalie's," Lulu concluded. "No other kids would have been around here today."

"That means she made it across the brook," said Pam.

"And didn't get dragged over the waterfall," Lulu added.

Anna patted Acorn's neck. "Good detective work, Acorn," she said.

"But where's Rosalie now?" Lulu wondered out loud.

They looked for more of Rosalie's footprints. But there was just that one.

Anna looked at how the deer prints led into the underbrush. The only way to walk through it was on a narrow path that the white-tailed deer made. "This run isn't wide enough or high enough for a riding trail," Anna told her friends. "But Rosalie wouldn't know that."

"And she probably doesn't know the difference between a deer's hoofprint and a horse's hoofprint," said Lulu. "She must have thought our ponies made these marks."

"I'll bet she went into the woods this way," Anna concluded. "I'll go through the deer run and look for her."

The girls decided that since Lulu knew the most about tracking, she should go with Anna and Acorn. And that Pam would stay behind with Snow White and Lightning to wait for Ms. Wiggins.

"Don't go too far," Pam warned. "And use your whistles if you need help."

The two girls and the pony entered the narrow, dark path.

"Rosalie," Anna called out. "Acorn is here to give you a ride. Where are you?"

"Rosalie," Lulu yelled. "If you hear us, shout back."

They stopped and listened. But all they heard was an owl's *who who-oo*.

The two girls and the pony came to a fork in the deer run. "Which way should we go?" Lulu asked.

Acorn snorted and pulled to his right. "Acorn thinks we should go this way," Anna told Lulu.

The girls took Acorn's advice and turned right. They walked slowly along the deer run looking for clues and calling for Rosalie.

Acorn pulled on the rein again. He wanted to move faster. Anna let him set the pace and the two girls kept up with him.

Acorn stopped abruptly. Had he found Rosalie? Anna looked at the tangled undergrowth to her right. No Rosalie. She looked to her left. No Rosalie. She looked straight ahead. A small figure in red shorts and a yellow T-shirt was coming around a turn in the path. Rosalie saw the two girls and Acorn at the same instant they saw her. She ran toward them.

Anna squatted and opened her arms to Rosalie. But Rosalie ran right past Anna and threw her arms around Acorn. "Oh, Acorn," she said in a hoarse whisper, "you found me."

Lulu and Anna smiled at each other. Then they raised their whistles to their lips and blew one short and one long blast.

Anna could see that Rosalie was scratched up and shivering with the cold. And she was speaking to Acorn in the raspy voice of someone whose voice is all worn out from shouting.

"Are you all right?" Lulu asked Rosalie.

Rosalie straightened herself up and said, "I'm okay. I went for a walk." She looked around the woods. "It's pretty in the woods."

Anna took her sweater out of the saddlebag and wrapped it around Rosalie's shivering shoulders. "I forgot my sweater," Rosalie whispered. "Thanks."

Anna and Lulu exchanged a glance. They both knew that when you rescue someone you have to be sure they aren't suffering from serious injuries or shock before you move them.

Anna sat on the pine-needle-covered path. "Sit down and we'll rest for a minute," she told Rosalie.

Rosalie sat down next to Anna. "I'm not tired," she said.

"It's six o'clock at night," Lulu said. "You've been walking in the woods all day. Your mother's been very worried about you. We've all been worried."

"Well, maybe I got a *little* lost," Rosalie said. Tears gathered in her eyes. She gulped to keep from crying. "But I wasn't scared."

Anna handed Rosalie her water bottle. "Don't drink it too fast," she cautioned.

While Rosalie drank the water and ate some trail mix, Anna carefully cleaned off her scratches with the antiseptic from the first-aid kit.

They all heard the *whacka whacka whacka* of a helicopter overhead. They looked up but couldn't see it through the cover of trees.

"I'll bet that's the state police," Lulu told Rosalie. "Looking for you."

"Is *everyone* looking for me?" Rosalie asked.

"*Everyone,*" Anna and Lulu both answered.

Rosalie opened her hand and Acorn bent over for a nibble of trail mix. "But Acorn's the one who found me," Rosalie said.

"Yeah," Anna told Rosalie. "Acorn found you. But don't give him any more trail mix, okay?"

"Okay," Rosalie said.

"But you could give him some water in your hand," Anna suggested.

"Okay," Rosalie said. She poured some water in her hand and held it out for the pony to lick.

"How would you like to ride out of the woods on Acorn?" Anna asked.

"Will it count as one of my two rides for when you get back from your camping trip?"

"No," Anna answered with a smile. "I'll still owe you two rides."

No More Ponies

Anna put her riding helmet on Rosalie and helped her mount Acorn. Then Anna took the reins and led her pony and his passenger along the deer run. "You might have to duck for some branches," Anna warned her. Rosalie leaned forward in the saddle, wrapped her arms loosely around Acorn's neck . . . and fell fast asleep.

Lulu walked on the other side of Acorn to be sure Rosalie didn't slip off the pony. But both Lulu and Anna could see how

careful Acorn was being with his special passenger.

When they came out at Badd Brook, Ms. Wiggins and Picasso were there waiting with Pam and the two ponies. Ms. Wiggins looked alarmed when she saw Rosalie slumped over Acorn. "What's happened to her?" she asked.

Anna smiled at Ms. Wiggins. "Rosalie's okay. She's just tired."

The Pony Pals and Ms. Wiggins led their horses along the trail back to the mansion. Ms. Wiggins said she'd heard their whistle blasts signaling that Rosalie had been found and was okay. "So I rode home and called town," she said. "Mrs. Lacey should know by now that her daughter is safe. She'll be very grateful to you girls for rescuing Rosalie."

Then the girls told Ms. Wiggins about the clues they'd put together to find Rosalie.

"You're real heros," Ms. Wiggins said. "The whole town should be proud of you."

"Acorn's a hero, too," Anna said.

*   *   *

The first thing Anna noticed as they approached the Wiggins mansion was that the town ambulance and a state trooper car were parked out front. The second thing she noticed was Mrs. Lacey running in their direction. The third thing she noticed was that Mike Lacey and Tommy Rand were right behind Mrs. Lacey.

Rosalie was awake now and sitting tall in the saddle. She waved to her mother. Mrs. Lacey called out, "Oh my baby. Oh my Rosalie." When she reached them, Mrs. Lacey told Ms. Wiggins, "Get my child off that animal." Anna heard anger in Mrs. Lacey's voice.

Ms. Wiggins helped Rosalie dismount Acorn and took off the riding helmet. Mrs. Lacey wrapped her little girl in her arms and hugged and kissed her. "Are you okay?" the tearful mother asked over and over.

During this mother-daughter reunion,

Mike Lacey and Tommy Rand came up to the Pony Pals. "You lost my sister," Mike accused. "You could have killed her."

"What do you expect from the Pony Pests?" Tommy Rand hissed.

Pam, Lulu, and Anna knew that they should just ignore them, but they couldn't ignore Mrs. Lacey.

"It's your fault that Rosalie got lost," Mrs. Lacey said to the Pony Pals. "You encouraged her to follow you. Why don't you play with kids your own age? You and those horses. You just leave my child alone."

"But Acorn *saved* me," Rosalie told her mother. "He *found* me."

"Hush," Mrs. Lacey told Rosalie. She put an arm around her daughter and pulled her close.

Ms. Wiggins tried to explain what really happened, but she was interrupted by the ambulance pulling up next to them. A medic hopped out of the front seat and two emergency medical team vounteers came out the back doors.

"Do I have to go the hospital, Mom?" Rosalie asked. "I'm not sick."

"We can start by checking her over here, ma'am," the medic told Mrs. Lacey.

The medic squatted in front of Rosalie. "You've had quite an adventure, young lady," he said. "I'll bet you're plenty thirsty."

Rosalie pointed to the Pony Pals. "They gave me lots of water," she said. "But I had to drink it slow. Acorn's the one who found me."

The medic opened his black medical bag. "I see some scratches that should be cleaned up here," he said.

"They already cleaned them," Rosalie told him.

The medic took a closer look at the scratches on Rosalie's arms and legs. Then he looked over at the Pony Pals. "Good work," he said. The Pony Pals smiled at each other. At least *somebody* appreciated them.

A few minutes later the medic said Rosalie was okay. "You can bring her right home," he told her mother. "But I'd keep her there for a day or two. Be sure she rests and takes plenty of fluids."

As the ambulance pulled away, Mrs. Lacey told Mike, "You'll have to stay with her tomorrow. I've got to work."

"But, Ma, I have a baseball game," he said.

Mrs. Lacey put her hands on her hips. "You will do what I say, Michael Lacey," she said. "Now get back in the police car. He said he'd bring us home."

Anna saw Mike mimic Mrs. Lacey behind her back. But he did what she said.

"Mom, I *can't* stay home," Rosalie informed her mother. "I've got *two* rides on Acorn to take. Two. I want one tomorrow."

Mrs. Lacey glared at the Pony Pals. "You promised her more rides?" Then she turned to Rosalie. "No pony rides. No more ponies. You are not to go near those girls. Or their horses. Do you understand?"

She grabbed Rosalie's hand, turned, and walked away. But not before Anna noticed that for the first time since she'd been found, Rosalie Lacey was crying.

A Letter for Acorn

Ms. Wiggins and the Pony Pals watched Mrs. Lacey and Rosalie get in the police car.

"I can't believe she's blaming us that Rosalie ran away and got lost," Lulu said.

"All we did was try to help," Pam said.

"She's being unfair," Anna added.

"I know," Ms. Wiggins said. "But Mrs. Lacey's too upset to listen to anyone right now. She's been through a lot."

"I just want to go back to our campsite," Anna told Pam and Lulu.

Ms. Wiggins looked to the west where the sun was dropping behind a ridge. "It'll be getting dark soon," she said. "You should hurry. I'll come along in a few minutes with the hot dogs and corn. We'll make a great campfire."

The Pony Pals and Ms. Wiggins had a delicious, fun-filled supper around the campfire. They cooked hot dogs on sticks. They roasted corn in the husks. For dessert they made sandwiches of toasted marsh-mallows and chocolate bars between graham crackers.

Ms. Wiggins said that the Pony Pals should be proud of what they did. If it hadn't been for them, Rosalie could still be lost.

"It's so dark tonight," Lulu said.

"And cold," said Pam as she drew closer to the warmth of the campfire.

After Ms. Wiggins and Picasso left, the three girls went to their tent.

Later, feeling cozy in her warm sleeping

bag, Anna looked up at the stars through the tent netting. She was happy that the Pony Pals were finally camping out. And she was happy that they'd found Rosalie and that she was okay.

Anna just wished she hadn't seen Rosalie cry. There must be something the Pony Pals could do to help her.

The next morning Anna was the first of the Pony Pals to wake up. She pulled the tent flap open and stuck her head out. A nighttime chill was still in the air and the ground was wet with dew. She saw that all three ponies were asleep standing up in the corral.

Anna lay there watching the ponies wake up and the morning brightening. Through the trees she saw three white-tailed deer drinking from the stream. And she watched a squirrel run up and down a tree with nuts to put away for winter. She even saw a garter snake slithering through the ground cover of dead leaves and pine needles.

Now Lulu and Pam woke up and the three girls fed the ponies and ate breakfast. The ponies had oats and grass. The girls had peanut butter and jelly sandwiches and orange juice.

The Pony Pals spent the morning following Ms. Wiggins' map of trail rides to the west. At noon they returned to the campsite to eat lunch and to pack up their equipment. Then they trail-rode home.

By four o'clock the three best friends and their ponies had reached Pony Pal Trail. It was time to say good-bye to Pam and Lightning.

"I guess our camping trip is officially over," Anna said.

They all agreed that their camping trip was one of the best Pony Pal times ever.

"But Rosalie being lost was scary," said Pam. "I'm really glad she wasn't injured or something."

They all agreed about that, too.

"I wonder if Rosalie will ever get a chance to ride again?" Lulu asked.

"Not until she doesn't live with her mother anymore," Anna said.

"I wish we could help her," said Pam.

"Me, too," Lulu added. "Maybe we should try to talk to her mother."

"Mrs. Lacey hates us," Anna said. "Especially me."

"This sounds like a Pony Pal Problem," said Pam.

"We need a plan," said Lulu. "Let's all think of what we can do so Rosalie can be with ponies again."

"We'll use our Pony Pal Power," Pam said.

"It'd be great if we could help Rosalie," said Anna.

Anna and Lulu said good-bye to Pam. As Anna rode home she thought of how sad she'd be if she couldn't be around ponies.

Lulu and Anna were bringing their ponies' bridles and saddles into the shelter when something caught Anna's eye. It was a plastic bag on top of the feed box. As she got closer, she saw two carrots and two apples in the bag. Under the bag was a folded piece of paper.

"It's a note or something," Lulu said.

Anna put down the tack she was carrying and picked up the note. She and Lulu read it together.

ACORN THANK YOU
I ♡ YOU
ROSALIE

"Poor Rosalie," Anna said. "Lulu, we've got to do something."

Three Ideas

The next morning the Pony Pals met in the Harley paddock to discuss what to do about Rosalie Lacey.

Pam showed Anna and Lulu her idea.

Rosalie should play with Jack and Jill instead of us.

"I talked to the twins about Rosalie," Pam said. "They know her from school.

She's a year older than they are, but they like her."

"If Rosalie played with Jack and Jill, she'd get to be around horses a lot," Lulu said.

"My mother knows Rosalie's mom from Parents Association at school," Pam said. "And my mother is going to Green Market this morning. To shop . . . and to invite Rosalie to play at our house."

"Great!" Anna said.

"Listen to my idea," Lulu said. She read:

We should talk to Mrs. Lacey.
No matter how mean she acts.

"We've got to get her to understand it wasn't our fault Rosalie ran away," Lulu said.

"But we shouldn't talk to her until *after* my mother's talked to her," Pam said.

"And no matter how Mrs. Lacey acts, we stick it out," Lulu said. "Right, Anna?"

Even though she was feeling angry and a little scared about talking to Mrs. Lacey, Anna agreed.

"What's *your* idea, Anna?" Lulu asked.

Anna showed her friends her idea.

Anna explained that her idea was to get Mrs. Lacey to let Rosalie ride Acorn again.

They all thought that Mrs. Lacey would probably let Rosalie play with the twins. Maybe she'd finally understand that it wasn't the Pony Pals' fault that Rosalie ran away. But how would they ever convince Mrs. Lacey to let Rosalie ride horses?

Around ten-thirty the three girls walked into the fruit and vegetable section of Green Market. Mrs. Lacey was unloading potatoes from a cloth sack into a bin. When she looked up and saw the Pony Pals, she frowned.

"Uh-oh," Anna groaned.

Mrs. Lacey finished dumping the potatoes and walked over to them. Anna was sure she was going to yell. She wanted to turn around and leave, but Lulu grabbed her arm.

Mrs. Lacey was still frowning when she told Pam that Rosalie was playing with the Crandal twins on Saturday. Anna couldn't figure out if Mrs. Lacey was angry at them or just nervous and shy.

"How is Rosalie feeling?" Pam asked her.

"She went back to day camp today," Mrs. Lacey said. She shifted uneasily from one foot to the other. "I want to thank you girls for finding Rosalie. I blamed you for her getting lost. But I know now that it was Mike's fault. He was supposed to bring her to day camp. Instead, he'd been letting her go alone."

The Pony Pals exchanged a glance. Mike's fault, not theirs. Anna could barely keep from smiling over that.

"The *County Times* called to ask me about Rosalie being lost," Mrs. Lacey said. "There's going to be an article saying you found her. You and your horses."

"Thank you," Lulu said.

"I'm glad you don't blame us anymore," said Pam.

"Rosalie's a nice kid," Anna said. "She's very smart and she's good with ponies."

"I guess just because I never liked horses doesn't mean Rosalie can't," Mrs. Lacey said. She finally smiled. Anna knew for sure that she'd just been nervous before. And maybe a little embarrassed about how she'd yelled at them the night of the rescue.

"Anyway, thanks again," Mrs. Lacey said. "Now I've got to get back to work."

When the Pony Pals were outside the store, Pam and Lulu raised their hands for high fives. But Anna held back.

"I forgot to do my idea," she said. "Wait here."

Anna ran back into the store. In a minute she came back out with a big smile on her face and told her friends. "She said yes! — Rosalie can ride."

The Pony Pals hit high fives and cheered, *"All right!"*

The next day was Saturday. At nine o'clock Mike brought Rosalie to the paddock, just as Anna had planned with Mrs. Lacey.

Acorn ran across the paddock to greet Rosalie. She gave him a big hug.

"Hi, Pony Pest," Mike said to Anna.

Rosalie glared at her brother. "Hey, quit

talking to my friend like that," she said, "or I'll tell Mom."

"Don't listen to him, Rosalie," Anna said.

"Pony Pals!" Mike said. "It's all so *stupid.*"

He turned and left the paddock. "Don't forget to pick me up at four o'clock," Rosalie called after him. "And don't be late."

When Mike was gone, Rosalie and Anna smiled at one another. "I like ponies better than boys," Rosalie said.

"Me, too," Anna said.

"I'm going to play with Jack and Jill Crandal," Rosalie said. "They like ponies."

"They *love* ponies," Anna said.

"My mom said you'd give me a ride today," said Rosalie.

"That's right," Anna said. "And a ride every week until school starts. Today, how would you like to ride over to the Crandals' on Pony Pal Trail?"

"Ride on the trail? What about you?" Rosalie asked.

"I get to ride Acorn lots," Anna said. "While you're playing with the twins, Acorn and I are going trail riding with Pam and Lulu. So you can ride Acorn all the way there."

"Yippee!" Rosalie said.

Anna pushed her fingers through Acorn's thick, black mane. She loved seeing Rosalie so happy. Acorn nickered and nudged Anna's shoulder.

Anna gave her pony a big hug and a kiss.

Too Many Ponies

For the original Pony Pal, Jean Feiwel

The author thanks Maria Genovesi, Elvia Gignoux, and Maria Nation for applying their knowledge of horses to this story.

Thanks also to Helen Perelman for her smart and sensitive editing.

Contents

Pam's New Job

Lightning was grazing under the big maple tree. "Hey, girl," Pam Crandal called. The pony looked up and trotted over to meet her. Lightning's chestnut coat was the same reddish-brown color as the autumn leaves on the maple tree.

The pony gently nudged Pam's shoulder and whinnied a hello. Pam rubbed Lightning's muzzle. "Good pony," she said.

Pam took an apple from her pocket and gave it to Lightning. While the pony ate the treat, Pam watched the two ponies in

the next paddock. Pam's mother was a riding instructor so there were always horses at the Crandals'. This year Mrs. Crandal had many young students and needed more ponies. Pam had gone with her mother to help pick out two ponies at Mr. Olson's horse farm. Pam was happy to see the ponies grazing in the paddock.

Lightning nudged at Pam's bulging jacket pocket. Pam rubbed the pretty white marking on her pony's forehead. "No more for you," she said. "Too many apples can make you sick."

Pam left Lightning and slipped through the fence rails into the next paddock. The two new ponies, Splash and Daisy, didn't come to greet her. And Pam didn't approach them. Instead she held out an apple in each hand and waited.

Splash trotted over to Pam, grabbed his apple, and returned to the other side of the field. Pam loved how the Appaloosa pony's markings on his back looked like splatters of paint.

Daisy, meanwhile, took cautious steps in Pam's direction. "Here, Daisy," Pam said to the little palomino Shetland. "This one's for you." Daisy came closer and lifted the apple daintily out of Pam's hand.

Pam's mother was watching from the fence. "I'm glad Splash and Daisy are getting to know you," she told Pam.

"It's fun to have them here," said Pam.

"I need you to work them with me," her mother said. "I'm too tall to ride them."

Pam remembered how she rode each of the ponies around Mr. Olson's riding ring while her mother watched. Pam and her mother agreed that both ponies were well-trained. But Pam knew that the ponies would need more schooling.

"We'll have to work them a lot before my young students ride them," Pam's mother explained. "I have many beginning riders this year."

Pam rubbed Daisy's golden-colored muzzle. "I'll help you, Mom," she said.

"I'll pay you," her mother said.

"Maybe I'll finally save enough money to buy a new saddle," said Pam.

Pam had been using a second-hand saddle for five years. The old saddle was looking worn-out and Pam wanted a new one. The saddle she'd seen at Mr. Olson's was perfect. It was shiny dark-brown leather, didn't have any worn spots, and was the perfect size for her and Lightning.

Mrs. Crandal interrupted Pam's saddle-thoughts. "We should start working Splash and Daisy this morning," she said. "Okay?"

"Sure," Pam said. "I was going trail riding with Anna and Lulu. But I'll tell them I can't go." Pam knew when her friends heard she had a job training ponies, they'd understand.

"Bring Splash to the barn in ten minutes then," Pam's mother said.

Pam sat on the fence between the two paddocks and did some math. How much had she already saved toward a saddle? How much more did she need for the beautiful one she'd seen at Mr. Olson's?

Pam stopped doing her math problem when she heard Lightning's happy neigh. She looked up and saw Anna and Lulu coming off the trail on their ponies, Acorn and Snow White.

Anna and Lulu dismounted their ponies and led them through the paddock gate. By then Lightning had reached them and the three ponies were nickering and nipping at one another happily.

Pam met her friends and their ponies halfway across the field.

"It's a perfect day for riding," Lulu told Pam.

"I can't wait to get on those Mudge Road trails," Anna said.

"Come see the new ponies first," said Pam.

When the three girls and their ponies reached the fence, Anna exclaimed, "They're so *cute!*"

"Daisy's a true palomino color," said Lulu.

"She's sweet, too," Pam told her friends. "They're both great ponies."

"How are they getting along with Lightning?" asked Lulu.

"We haven't put them together yet," Pam said. "But they've been visiting over the fence."

"I think Lightning would rather be with Snow White and Acorn," said Anna.

Pam agreed with Anna. Like the Pony Pals, their three ponies were best friends. Pam rubbed Lightning's long, sleek neck. "You'll be with Acorn and Snow White tonight," she told her pony. "We're having a barn sleepover."

"They'll be together all day, too," Lulu reminded Pam, "while we're trail riding. So let's go. Saddle up."

"I'm going to help my mother work with the new ponies," Pam said. "And guess what? She's going to pay me. I'll have enough money for a new saddle a lot sooner than I thought. And Mr. Olson's got one for sale that's perfect for me. It's used, but it looks like new."

The Pony Pals hit high fives all around and shouted, "All right!"

"My job starts today," Pam said. "So I can't go riding with you."

"But we planned it," Anna said. "We're going on the Mudge Road trails."

"My dad told me about an old town that used to be over there," Lulu said. "We're going to look for the places the houses used to be."

At that moment, Pam's mother shouted to her from the barn. "Pam, catch Splash and bring him in. We'll work him first."

"Okay," Pam called back.

"We could wait for you," Lulu said.

"I've got two ponies to work," Pam said. "It'll be a long time."

"You mean you can't trail ride at all today?" Anna said.

Pam nodded.

"So I guess we'll go without you," Lulu said unhappily.

"But you'll be back here later," Pam reminded her friends, "for supper and our barn sleepover. We'll have fun."

"Sure," Anna said.

"See you later," said Lulu.

Lulu and Anna led their ponies out onto Riddle Road, and Pam went to fetch the new pony. She was thinking about how she would catch Splash, when she heard Lightning snort. She looked across the paddock. Lightning was pounding up and down the fence line bordering Riddle Road. The pony snorted again. What was wrong with Lightning?

Left Behind

Pam ran across the paddock. "Lightning. Lightning, it's okay," she called to the pony.

The unhappy pony ignored Pam and kept rushing up and down the fence line. Pam could see that Lightning wanted to go with Acorn and Snow White.

Even the family dog, Woolie, knew Lightning was upset. Woolie wasn't running alongside Lightning the way he usually did. Instead, he sat next to Pam, whimpering. Pam patted the dog's head and told him that everything would be all right.

When Anna and Lulu and their ponies were out of sight, Lightning finally stopped carrying on and slowly walked over to Pam.

Pam lay her head against her pony's hot side. She heard and felt Lightning's heart-beat racing. "I'm sorry," she said.

Lightning looked toward Riddle Road and neighed.

"I know," Pam said. "They're my best friends, too. We'll all be together tonight."

As Pam comforted her pony, she thought about her Pony Pals, Anna Harley and Lulu Sanders.

Pam and Anna met in kindergarten. On that first day of school, Anna had finger-painted a big red and yellow pony. Pam told Anna she was the best artist in the class. They talked about ponies the whole day. And became best friends.

Pam knew how lucky she was that her parents loved ponies as much as she did. Her mother taught horseback riding and her father was a veterinarian. And Pam had a pony for as long as she could remember. But Anna didn't have a pony until she was ten. Which was around the time that Pam and Anna met Lulu Sanders and Snow White.

Lulu came to Wiggins to live with her grandmother while her father studied animals in far-off places. But now Mr. Sanders was in Wiggins writing an article about black bears. Pam was glad Lulu and her father were together again. Lulu's mother died when she was little, and Lulu and her dad were especially close.

Anna and Lulu kept their ponies in a paddock behind Anna's house. A mile-and-a-half woodland trail — Pony Pal Trail — connected that paddock to Lightning's paddock at the Crandals'. So it was easy for the Pony Pals to visit one another on horseback.

Pam saw her mother waving to her from the barn doorway. "Haven't you caught Splash yet?" she yelled.

"Coming," Pam shouted back.

Pam looked into Lightning's eyes. Her pony had calmed down and was breathing normally again. "I'm sorry you can't be with your friends," she told Lightning. "But I've got a job. Pretty soon we'll have enough money for a new saddle for us. You'll love that."

Splash was standing at the fence between the paddocks waiting for Lightning. Pam thought she'd have trouble catching Splash. But with Lightning beside her it would be easy.

While the two ponies sniffed each other, Pam slipped through the fence and clipped a lead rope on Splash's halter. She reached over and she patted Lightning's cheek. "Thanks for helping," she said. Then she led Splash to the barn.

Pam knew she had to forget about Lightning now. If she was going to school Splash, she had to give him all of her attention. Pam talked gently to Splash and gave him friendly pats while she groomed and saddled him.

When Pam led the new pony outside, she saw her mother waiting for her in the center of the outdoor ring. Pam swung herself up on Splash's back.

"Start with a walk," Mrs. Crandal directed.

Everything went fine during the walk. But when Pam was doing a posting trot, she felt that her stirrups weren't right. She moved Splash back down to a walk, then brought him to a halt. "I need to lengthen my stirrups," she told her mother.

Mrs. Crandal and Pam were adjusting Pam's stirrups when the five-year-old Crandal twins, Jack and Jill, came running over to them.

"Can I ride Splash?" Jack asked.

"Me, too?" Jill said.

"I have to work him before any kids ride him," Pam told them.

"What have you been doing?" Mrs. Crandal asked the twins.

"Chasing mice," Jill said.

"Isn't that a job for the barn cats?" their mother asked.

"They're sleeping," Jack said.

"Where did you see mice?" Pam wanted to know.

"In the feed room," said Jill.

"I noticed some droppings in there this morning," Pam told her mother. "I think Jezebel and No Tail are bored with catching mice."

"I think they've turned into lazy cats," Mrs. Crandal said. "Maybe after all these years they've retired." She sighed. "But we'll worry about that later. Right now, let's get back to work with Splash."

The twins left the ring and Pam worked Splash in a walk and trot. When she directed the pony to go back to a walk, Splash continued to trot. Pam was firm with the pony and he finally slowed down.

"Good work, Pam," her mother said. "You're great at this."

"Thanks," Pam said.

Pam noticed Lightning standing at the

fence staring at her. Is Lightning jealous that I'm riding Splash? she wondered.

Just then a truck going along Riddle Road backfired. Splash was spooked by the sudden noise and stumbled. Pam lost her balance for a split second. But she caught herself and regained balance as she reined in the frightened pony.

"Pam," her mother scolded, "you need to stay focused."

"Sorry," Pam said.

I have to stop worrying about Lightning, Pam thought. I've got to pay attention to my job.

Fat Cat

After lunch, Pam went back out to the paddocks to get Daisy for *her* lesson. When Pam called out "Daisy," the pony looked in Pam's direction and took a step backward. She's very shy, Pam thought. I hope she's not hard to catch. Pam put her hand behind her back so Daisy wouldn't see she was carrying a lead rope.

Meanwhile, Lightning was getting as close to Pam as possible. She stuck her muzzle through the fence rails and nudged at the lead rope and nickered. To Pam, Lightning seemed to be saying, "Don't take that other pony. Take me."

"Sorry, Lightning," she said, "I *have* to ride Daisy. It's my job."

Pam talked quietly to Daisy and the pony stayed still for her. Pam clipped the lead rope to Daisy's halter and led her toward the barn. Lightning followed them to the gate.

After Daisy's lesson, Pam sat on the fence and pushed her fingers through Lightning's red mane. Pam knew that her new job was confusing Lightning. "And you miss Acorn and Snow White," Pam said. "Now that I'm finished working for today, I miss them, too."

Pam kept looking over to Riddle Road. Soon two ponies and their riders came into view.

"They're back," she told Lightning excitedly. "Let's go meet them."

Pam tied the lead rope to Lightning's halter and heaved herself on her bare back. Lightning nickered happily, stretched out her sleek body, and cantered toward the paddock gate.

As Pam slid off Lightning's back she saw that a big gray cat was walking beside Acorn and Anna.

"Where'd that cat come from?" Pam asked.

"We found him on Mudge Road," Lulu said.

"It's the biggest cat I've ever seen," Pam said.

"He followed us," said Anna. "But something's wrong with his leg. He limps. We thought your dad should look at him."

Pam picked up the cat and stroked its soft gray coat. "He's so furry," she said.

"And fat," Lulu added.

While Anna and Lulu unsaddled their ponies, Pam put the cat in the barn office. Then she went to get her dad from the animal clinic.

By the time Pam and Dr. Crandal came into the barn, Anna, Lulu, Jack, Jill, Mrs. Crandal, and Woolie were crowded in the

office. The gray cat, sitting on Mrs. Crandal's desk chair, was the center of everyone's attention.

"Well," Dr. Crandal said, "what have we here?"

"A cat," said Jill. "Anna and Lulu found him. He doesn't have a tag."

"His name is Fat Cat," Jack announced. "I named him."

"Me, too!" Jill added.

"Well, Mr. Fat Cat," Dr. Crandal said, "let's take a look at you." Dr. Crandal picked up the cat and checked him over. "She's purring like a motorboat," he said with a smile.

" 'She'?" Pam said with surprise. "He's a she?"

"Fat Cat is not only a female cat," Dr. Crandal told them, "she's a pregnant cat."

"Pregnant means she's going to have kittens," Pam told Jill.

"I *know* that," Jill said.

"What about her leg?" Anna asked.

"Her leg is a little swollen," Dr. Crandal

said. "She must have sprained it. But it's nothing to worry about. It's the sort of injury that fixes itself."

"What are we going to do with another cat?" Mrs. Crandal wondered out loud. "And then kittens!"

Fat Cat suddenly jumped out of Dr. Crandal's arms and raced around the room.

"Look!" Anna squealed. "She's chasing a mouse."

"I see it!" Lulu shouted. "It's going under the door."

Mrs. Crandal quickly opened the door. The cat streaked out of the office to continue the chase down the barn aisle. Woolie cheered Fat Cat on with an enthusiastic bark.

Everyone laughed.

"Fat Cat," Mrs. Crandal said, "you've got yourself a job."

"And a new home," Pam added.

After a spaghetti dinner with the Crandals, the three friends went out to the barn.

119

They got the tack room ready for their sleepover by laying out their sleeping bags side by side. Then they went out and sat on the fence.

The paddocks were lit by the white light of a full moon. The Pony Pals watched Acorn and Lightning trot toward the big maple tree. Snow White followed at a slower pace. When the faster ponies reached the tree, they turned around and went back to get Snow White.

"They're great friends," Anna remarked. "Just like us."

Meanwhile Daisy and Splash grazed at the far side of their own paddock. Pam told Anna and Lulu about her training sessions with Splash and Daisy. "I'm getting to know them," she said. "Splash has lots of energy. But I think he's used to getting away with stuff."

"What about the Shetland?" Anna asked. "Is Daisy a lot like Acorn?"

"She's sweet like Acorn," said Pam, "so

I think she'll be great with little kids. But she's lazy and slow. My job is to get her to work harder."

Pam wanted to keep talking about her job and the saddle she was going to buy with the money she made. But Lulu changed the subject. "We found the neatest place today," she said.

"Wait until you see it, Pam," Anna said. "It's ancient. We went where Lulu's dad said there once was a farm. And we found where a house used to be."

"There's a big hole in the ground with rock walls," Lulu said. "It used to be a cellar."

"We explored in there for the longest time," Anna added. "I want to go back and dig in the ground. I bet we'll find pieces of stuff they used in that house."

"We'll go tomorrow," Lulu told Pam, "and show you."

"I can't," Pam said. "I'm working with the new ponies."

"*Again!*" Anna wailed. "That's awful."

"That means you're not riding with us at all this weekend," Lulu complained.

"I can't help it," Pam said.

The three girls were silent. After a while they went to the barn and got ready for bed. Pam was the first to get into her sleeping bag. Suddenly she jumped up screaming. "Some*thing* — is — in — there," she stuttered.

The Pony Pals ran to the door. They stared at the sleeping bag. It moved.

"What is it?" Anna whispered.

"Maybe it's a racoon," Lulu said.

They saw a bit of fur at the opening of the sleeping bag. Then more fur. A big gray cat crawled all the way out.

"Fat Cat!" the girls squealed.

Fat Cat looked around as if to ask, "What's all the fuss about?"

The Pony Pals ran back into the room and collapsed in a giggling heap on top of Pam's sleeping bag. Fat Cat rubbed against them, swished her furry tail, and purred.

Pam was still giggling when she picked up the cat and put her in the feed room. "You have work to do tonight, Fat Cat," she said. "Go scare mice instead of people." She closed the door to the tack room so Fat Cat wouldn't come back to the barn sleepover party.

The girls got settled in their sleeping bags. "I wish you could come with us tomorrow, Pam," Lulu said.

"I thought being Pony Pals meant we rode together," said Anna.

Pam didn't say anything. She was thinking about how much she liked her job training Splash and Daisy.

Splash's Trail Ride

Every day after school for a week, Pam worked the new ponies in the ring. She was very tired. But when Pam heard Woolie's bark early Saturday morning, she jumped right out of bed anyway. She wanted to get her barn chores done early today. This morning and all weekend she was going riding with her friends.

Pam walked out to the paddock where Lightning and the two new ponies had spent the night. All three ponies came running toward her. Lightning reached her first. While Pam gave her pony a special good-morning hug, Splash came over and tried to nudge his way between Lightning and Pam. Pam gave him a friendly pat on the muzzle. Then she turned her attention to Daisy who waited shyly behind the other two ponies.

Pam went to the feed room to get oats. The enormous gray cat was sitting on the feed box, alert to every little movement and sound. There isn't a mouse in Wiggins who would dare to enter this room, Pam thought.

Pam scratched the cat behind the ears. "Good job, Fat Cat," she said. Fat Cat purred her thanks, then jumped off the feed box so Pam could open it.

When Pam had finished feeding the ponies, she checked the chart she'd made for schooling Splash. She needed to make sure that Splash would be ready for her mother's students.

TRAINING CHART
SPLASH

NW = needs work
G = good
VG = very good

	Sa	Su	M	T	W	Th	F
stands still for mount	G	G	G	VG	VG	VG	VG
halt	NW	G	VG	VG	NW	G	VG
walk	G	G	G	G	G	G	G
trot	G	G	VG	VG	VG	VG	VG
canter	VG	VG	VG	VG	VG	VG	VG
jumps	—	—	—	G	G	VG	VG
transitions	NW	NW	NW	NW	NW	G	G
on trail alone	—	—	—	—	—	—	VG
on trail in group	—	—	—	—	—	—	—

comments spooked when truck backfired   doesn't like to slow down   needs to ride on trail with other ponies

Pam saw that she needed to take Splash trail riding in a group. If I take Splash out today with my friends, she thought, I'd be working and playing at the same time. Her mother agreed with the plan.

A few minutes later, Pam led Lightning to the barn. Instead of tacking her up, she put her in a stall in the back. "I know you like it better outside," she said. "But you'll only be here for a little while."

Pam returned to the paddock, caught Splash, and saddled him up. She asked her mother to let Lightning out after she left. "Lightning would be so upset that I'm trail riding on Splash instead of her," she explained.

"I'll put her back out in the paddock with Daisy as soon as you're out of sight," her mother promised. "And remember," she added, "stick to Pony Pal Trail until you're sure Splash is okay riding in a group."

As Pam rode Splash along the trail, she noticed how much the pony had improved in the one week she'd been working with him. Now when she asked him to slow down he responded quickly. And when a squirrel streaked across the trail he didn't spook.

Pam couldn't believe she could be having so much fun and getting paid for it! "You're a terrific little pony," she told Splash. "And you're a good ride."

Pam was the first to reach the Pony Pal meeting place at the three white birch trees. She hadn't told Anna and Lulu that she'd be riding Splash instead of Lightning. But she knew they'd understand. Working Splash on the trail was part of her job.

When Snow White and Acorn appeared around the bend of the trail, Anna said, "Where's Lightning?"

"Is she sick?" asked Lulu.

"Lightning's fine," Pam said. "I have to work Splash on the trail with other ponies."

Splash whinnied and pulled up against the bit. Pam pulled him in sharply. "He doesn't usually do that," she said. "We better stick to Pony Pal Trail for awhile."

"Then let's go back to that old town," Anna said.

Lulu patted the short shovel she'd tied to the back of her saddle. "We'll do a dig," she said, "like archaeologists."

"I have to stick around here with Splash," Pam said. "We haven't checked him on a road with cars yet. We can bring him over there another time."

"Aren't you ever going to ride Lightning again?" Anna asked.

"Of course," Pam said. "Lightning's my pony. But right now I *have* to ride Splash."

Acorn pawed at the ground restlessly. Snow White neighed. They missed Lightning, too.

"We'd better get these ponies moving," said Lulu.

"Lulu, it's your turn to take the lead," Pam said.

Lulu directed Snow White to move forward.

Anna followed on Acorn.

Pam and Splash took up the rear.

Lulu started them out at a walk, but Splash immediately wanted to trot. When Pam tried to hold him in the walk, he did a jig in place. It was as difficult to hold him back as on the first day she worked him.

"Come on, Splash," Pam scolded, "behave yourself."

Splash's ears went back, and he scooted. In a split second he'd covered the space between himself and Acorn. Acorn whinnied his disapproval and tried to turn on Splash. Anna struggled to keep Acorn in check. Meanwhile, Splash was tossing his head and snorting.

"Don't let him crowd," Anna shouted to Pam as she finally got Acorn to move forward again. "Keep the space between them."

"Sorry," Pam said. "Maybe if you guys go a little faster it'll work better."

Lulu moved Snow White through a trot into a canter. Acorn followed at the same speed. But Splash still strained to go faster than the ponies ahead of him.

"*Whoa!*" Pam shouted at the pony. She pulled hard on the reins until Splash finally stopped. "That's enough," she scolded.

Pam was panting hard from the effort of controlling Splash and she felt the sweat under the rim of her hat. Splash was breathing hard and sweating, too.

All three girls dismounted. Lulu walked over to Pam while Anna held Acorn and Snow White a safe distance away from Splash.

"This is a bad idea," Lulu told Pam. "It's dangerous for us to ride with Splash."

"He was *perfect* yesterday," Pam said.

"Why don't you bring him back and get Lightning," Lulu suggested. "Then the day won't be ruined. We'll wait for you."

"If I put Splash out in the paddock for the rest of the day he'll think it's a reward for his bad behavior," Pam explained. "Then he'll be even worse the next time he goes on the trail with other horses."

"Promise you won't bring Splash the next time we ride," Anna said.

"I promise," Pam told her.

"Good!" Lulu said. "Then maybe things will go back to normal."

Pam hoped that she could keep her promise to her friends and her job.

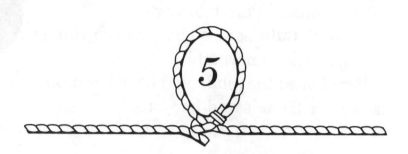

The Fight

Sunday morning Mrs. Crandal handed Pam her first week's salary. After breakfast Pam ran up to her room and took her barn bank down from the top bookshelf. She opened the roof, took out the money she'd already saved, and counted it. Great, she thought, if I work every day pretty soon I'll have enough for that new saddle.

Pam walked into the kitchen to find her mother. "I want to work today, too," Pam told her.

"I thought we'd all take today off," Mrs. Crandal said.

"But I haven't ridden Daisy on the trail yet," Pam said.

"What about Lightning?" Mrs. Crandal asked. "I thought you were taking her out today."

"I can ride her when I get back," Pam said.

After Pam put Lightning in a stall in the back of the barn, she went to the front to groom and saddle up Daisy.

Daisy nickered cheerfully when Pam rode her onto Pony Pal Trail. The palomino pony seemed to be saying, "I like it here. This is a very pretty place." She liked the trail so much that she wanted to stop to admire every falling leaf and chirping bird. Pam let the pony take her time so she'd get used to the trail. She figured Daisy would happily move into the trot and canter when she was behind fast-moving Acorn and Snow White.

Pam saw Anna and Lulu waiting for her at their birch tree meeting place. She waved and they waved back. But Anna was frowning and Lulu was twisting her mouth the way she did when she was angry.

"Why didn't you tell us you were riding Daisy today?" Anna asked as Pam rode up to her.

"I didn't decide until this morning," Pam said.

"Don't let Daisy get too close to Snow White," Lulu ordered.

"Daisy won't act like Splash did yesterday," Pam said. "Stop worrying."

Acorn took a step forward and nickered a friendly hello to Daisy.

"See," said Pam. "They like Daisy. She'll be great with them on the trail. And she'll never try to rush ahead like Splash did."

"Lightning must hate that you keep leaving her behind," said Anna.

"She doesn't know," Pam said. "I put her in the barn, then my mom lets her out when I'm gone."

"I bet Lightning still knows," Lulu said. "She's smart. You can't fool her."

Pam didn't want to feel guilty about Lightning. She was riding Daisy today and it was Daisy she had to think about. "Let's just ride, okay?" she said.

The three girls moved their ponies onto the trail. Anna was in the lead. Lulu came next. Pam and Daisy brought up the rear.

When the ponies walked, everything was fine. "I told you she'd be okay," Pam shouted ahead to her friends.

Anna moved Acorn into a lively trot. Snow White followed. But Daisy had a slower trot and soon she was lagging behind. When the other ponies cantered, Daisy fell even farther behind.

I have to let Daisy know what I want and be firm, Pam reminded herself. She gave all her attention to the lazy pony, but it didn't make much difference.

By the time Pam caught up with her Pony Pals they had reached Badd Brook. Anna and Lulu were sitting on a big rock and having a snack while their ponies were drinking from the brook.

"Daisy is such a slowpoke," Pam said as she led the pony to the stream.

"She sure is different from Splash," said Lulu.

"And Lightning," Anna added. "I miss Lightning."

"What should we do next?" Lulu asked.

"I wanted to go back to that old house," Anna said. "But I guess we can't with Daisy."

"There's plenty to do around here," Pam said. "We always have fun on the Wiggins Estate trails."

"I just hate it when we plan something and then can't do it," complained Lulu.

No one said anything for awhile.

Anna finished her snack and brushed the crumbs off her jacket. "It's like you're not even a Pony Pal anymore," she mumbled.

"Anna, that's a dumb thing to say," said Pam. "Why'd you say that?"

"Because you're forgetting all about

Lightning," Anna said. "And the Pony Pals."

"And you keep doing things without telling us," said Lulu. "Like bringing these other ponies on our rides."

"And then we can't do what we said we'd do. Like going to that old farm," Anna said.

"I have a job," Pam said in an angry voice. "I can't *play* all the time like you."

"Pam, you're working too hard," Lulu said. "You never just have fun anymore."

Pam jumped up. "You guys are jealous that I have a job and you don't," she said.

"That's ridiculous," said Lulu. "I am not jealous."

"Me either," Anna said. "Who'd want to turn into a grump like you?"

"I'm not a grump," shouted Pam. "You guys are the grumps. You're the ones who are complaining all the time. You're the ones who are being selfish and mean!"

Anna folded her arms and turned her back to Pam. Lulu picked up some pebbles and started thowing them, one by one, into the water.

Pam wanted to get away from Anna and Lulu as fast as she could. She ran over to Daisy and put on the bridle. Anna and Lulu still ignored her. Pam mounted the pony. "Now you can go play in that stupid old house," she told them.

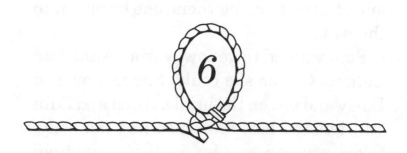

Keep Away

Pam rode through the woods toward Pony Pal Trail. She wanted to get far away from her *former* friends. But Daisy was the slowest pony she ever rode.

Lightning would be thrilled to move into a gallop. It was much more fun to ride her own pony. On Lightning she would feel as if she were *flying* over the open stretch of trail.

When Pam reached the paddock gate, she saw that her pony was in the run-in shed at the other end of the field. She took the long way to the barn so Lightning wouldn't see her on another pony.

Pam took off Daisy's tack and cooled her down. She couldn't wait to finish with this pony so she could take Lightning for a ride on Pony Pal Trail.

But thinking about the trail reminded her of the good times she had riding with Anna and Lulu.

Pam thought about their ponies' happy whinnies and the sound of hooves pounding along the trail. She remembered their Pony Pal adventures and some of the difficult problems they'd solved together. Mostly she remembered how special and wonderful it felt to be a Pony Pal.

Why did Anna and Lulu have to go ruin the Pony Pals by being jealous? Pam was so angry at Anna and Lulu that she wanted to scream.

After putting Daisy in the side paddock with Splash, Pam went to get Lightning. She and Lightning would go for a ride alone. She didn't need Pony Pals. She had her pony. "Lightning," Pam called. "Come on, girl. We're going for a ride!"

But Lightning didn't come out of the shed. She didn't even turn around.

As Pam got closer she shouted, "Hey, Lightning, it's me. Pam. Didn't you hear me?"

Lightning still didn't turn around.

"We're going for a ride," Pam repeated.

Pam suddenly felt frightened. Even when her pony was munching on grass or hay, she always looked in the direction of Pam's voice.

Pam took a step into the shed. Lightning turned her head, put her ears back, and bared her teeth. It was the fiercest look Pam had ever seen on any pony's face. She was so startled by it that she let out a frightened yelp and ran out of the shed. Her heart pounded. What's wrong with my pony? she wondered. Is she angry at me?

I have to get help, Pam told herself.

First she ran to her father's animal clinic.

No one was there.

She ran to the house. As she burst into the kitchen she screamed. "Mom! Dad! Help! Something's wrong with Lightning."

Nobody answered her call. She ran upstairs. No one was there.

She decided to check her mother's office in the barn. As Pam was leaving the house through the kitchen she noticed a note on the table.

Pam, dear —
Dad and I took the twins
to the Danbury Mall to get
shoes. Back around five.
              Love,
              Mom

Pam's heart sank. There was no one to help her. She had to face this problem alone. If only Anna and Lulu hadn't ruined the Pony Pals, she thought. If only we didn't have a fight. . . .

She ran back to the run-in shed. Lightning still had her back to her. Pam spoke to Lightning in a calm, soothing voice. "Did I wake you up from a nightmare before?" she asked. "Well, everything's okay now. Let's go for a ride."

Lightning ignored her.

Pam stepped into the shed and the horrible thing happened again. Lightning turned on her with fierce eyes, bared teeth, and an angry snort.

Pam didn't scream this time. She knew that if she was going to figure out what was wrong with Lightning she had to remain calm.

The first question she asked herself was, "Is Lightning sick?"

Pam knew what Lightning looked like when she was sick and she didn't look like that now. Lightning's head wasn't drooping. Her coat didn't look feverish.

So if she isn't sick, Pam wondered, what's wrong? Then she remembered what Anna said, "Lightning must hate that you keep leaving her behind." And how Lulu said, "Lightning's smart. You can't fool her."

Pam also remembered the way Lightning stood watching at the fence the first time she rode Splash. What if Lightning knows that I'm taking Splash and Daisy out on the trail instead of her? Pam thought. She must be jealous. And now she's angry.

"I'm sorry I've been riding Splash and Daisy so much," Pam told Lightning. "And I'm sorry I didn't take you on the trail this weekend." Pam felt the tears streaming down her face. "Please forgive me."

Lightning whipped her tail around in a circle and snorted.

For the first time in her life Pam was afraid of her own pony.

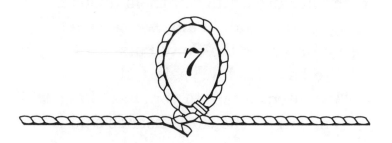

Crazy Pony

Pam sat on the grass near the shed and wiped the tears away with her shirtsleeve. She stared at Lightning. Her pony had gone crazy because she hadn't given her enough attention. Pam wished with all her heart that her friends were there to help her.

Then she heard Acorn's whinny and her friends' voices. At first she thought she was imagining them. But she saw that Anna and Lulu were really there, leading their ponies across the paddock.

Pam ran up to them. Before she could

catch her breath to tell them about Lightning, Anna said. "Pam, we can't let *anything* break up the Pony Pals."

"We have to talk," said Lulu.

"I wanted to talk to you, too," Pam said.

"I'm sorry!" the three friends said in unison.

Lulu and Anna were so happy that the fight was over that they laughed out loud. But their laughter stopped when they looked at Pam. "Something's wrong with Lightning," Pam said.

"What happened?" Anna asked.

"I was going to ride her," Pam began, "but Lightning, she . . . she's so mad at me. She won't leave the shed. It's like she's turned into a crazy pony! And it's all my fault."

"Start at the beginning and tell us everything," Lulu said.

While they led Acorn and Snow White to a side paddock, Pam told her friends everything that Lightning had done since she got home.

When Pam finished, Anna said, "Don't worry, Pam. We'll help you. We're Pony Pals. We have Pony Pal Power."

Then the three friends ran over to the shed. They observed Lightning and thought about what to do next.

"Here's an idea," said Lulu. "If Lightning is mad at you, maybe I should get her."

"Good thinking," Pam said. She handed the halter and lead rope to Lulu.

"Hi, Lightning," Lulu said as she walked toward her. "It's time to come out. Snow White's in the other paddock. She wants to play with you."

"Be careful, Lulu," Anna warned. "Go around so she can't kick you."

The moment Lulu stepped into the shed, Lightning turned on her with a fierce, angry look.

Lulu backed quickly away. "Sorry, Lightning," she said in a trembling voice.

"Lightning doesn't even look like Lightning," Anna said. "This is awful!"

"She won't let us near her," Lulu said.

"We'll have to get her to leave on her own," Anna said.

"But how?" Lulu asked.

"Food," said Pam. "Maybe she'll leave the shed for oats."

They all agreed that it was a good idea.

Pam ran to the barn. In a few minutes she was back with oats and carrots. She placed the bucket of oats at the edge of the shed. "Lightning, here's some good oats for you," she said in a cheery voice.

Lightning turned toward the sound of Pam's voice and sniffed the air for the sweet smell of oats.

"It's going to work," Anna whispered.

But at that instant, Lightning turned back toward the shed wall.

Pam moved the bucket of oats into the shed. Lightning kicked out at her with a back leg.

Pam ran to Anna and Lulu. "Lightning *never* kicks," she told them. "It's like she's turned into another pony. A mean one."

"Let's look at what we've figured out so far," Lulu suggested.

"Lightning won't let us in the shed," said Pam.

"And she won't come out," Lulu said.

"Maybe we should give her something to eat without going in," said Anna. "If we put a carrot on a stick we wouldn't have to go in the shed and she wouldn't have to leave."

"It's worth a try," Lulu agreed.

Pam broke a dead branch off the maple tree while Lulu unlaced one of her shoes. Anna used the shoelace to tie the carrot loosely to the end of the branch. Then Anna dangled the carrot out where Lightning could smell it. "Here's a treat for you, Lightning," she said.

Lightning turned her head toward Anna. But this time she didn't make the terrible face. Instead she quickly pulled the carrot off the branch. The girls let out sighs of relief.

"Well, now we're getting somewhere," said Lulu.

"Maybe you should try to go in now," Anna whispered to Pam, "while she's eating the carrot."

"But keep away from her legs," warned Lulu as she handed the halter and lead rope back to Pam.

Pam took a few steps into the shed before Lightning noticed her. But when she did, the pony dropped the carrot so she could snort angrily at Pam.

Pam rushed out of the shed. "Nothing we try is working," she told her friends.

"Don't give up, Pam," said Lulu. "We never give up."

"It's all my fault," said Pam.

"Maybe Lightning isn't mad at you," Anna said. "Maybe there's another reason she wants to stay in the shed."

"Maybe there's something in the shed that would keep her in there," added Lulu.

"Then we have to figure out what it is," Pam said

"Maybe there's a poisonous snake in the

straw," Anna said. "And Lightning is protecting us from getting bit."

"Then why hasn't *she* been bit?" asked Lulu.

"Maybe she *has* been bit," Pam said with alarm. "And that's why she's acting so weird."

"She doesn't have a swollen leg or anything," said Lulu. "And she's standing so still. I think she'd be jumping all over the place if she got bit."

Just then Fat Cat came walking by the girls. She was headed toward the shed.

"Catch her," Anna yelled. "Lightning's acting so crazy she might step on her."

But Fat Cat was already under the legs of the angry pony.

"Come back, Fat Cat!" Pam yelled.

The Baby-sitter

Anna wanted to run into the shed to save the cat from the dangerous pony. But Lulu grabbed Anna's arm and held her back.

Meanwhile, the pony stayed perfectly still and calm. Lightning didn't snort at the cat. She didn't make an angry face. She didn't kick.

"Maybe it's just people she won't let go in the shed," said Lulu.

Pam crouched down. "Look," she said, "Fat Cat's digging at the straw."

Anna and Lulu squatted beside Pam to watch what happened next. Fat Cat went deeper into the straw until all they could see was the end of her fluffy tail.

"Something's in that straw," said Lulu.

"Maybe it's mice," said Pam.

"Did you notice that Fat Cat doesn't look so fat anymore?" asked Anna.

"Kittens!" the Pony Pals said in unison.

"That must be it," said Anna. "Fat Cat's had her babies in there."

They waited quietly to see what would happen next.

"Oh-hh, look," Pam whispered.

Fat Cat walked out of the shed between Lightning's legs. She held a tiny kitten in her mouth.

"It's true!" Pam cried. "Lightning was protecting Fat Cat's kittens!"

"And she didn't want us to step on them by mistake," said Lulu.

"Let's follow Fat Cat and see where she puts the kittens," said Anna.

"I hope she doesn't hide them," Lulu said. "Some mother cats like to be private."

"Let's set up a box and food for her in the feed room closet," said Pam. "It's private in there."

"I hope it works," said Lulu.

Anna and Pam ran toward the barn. Lulu followed Fat Cat.

Pam laid an old blanket in an empty cardboard box and put it in the closet. Anna put a bowl of cat food and fresh water near the door to the feed room Then they went into an empty stall to watch.

A few seconds later Fat Cat walked into the barn, still carrying the tiny kitten. Lulu was spying on her from a safe distance. Fat Cat walked right by the feed room. Pam and Anna mouthed "Oh, no" to one another.

Suddenly, Fat Cat turned around and marched right back to the feed room.

Lulu went into the stall with Pam and Anna. In a few seconds they saw Fat Cat

leave the feed room. There wasn't a kitten in her mouth.

The Pony Pals hit silent high fives. Then they tiptoed into the feed room to take a peek at the newborn kitten.

"It looks like a baby mouse," Anna whispered. "It's so tiny."

"I wonder how many more there'll be," said Lulu.

"Let's go back and watch," suggested Pam.

The Pony Pals sat in the grass by the shed and watched as, one by one, Fat Cat pulled her kittens out of the straw and carried them to the barn. Between kitten number 2 and kitten number 3 Lightning turned her head to the Pony Pals. Her ears were relaxed, her teeth didn't show, and her eyes were calm.

"She trusts us now," said Lulu.

"And she's not mad at me," added Pam.

When Fat Cat scampered away from the

shed with kitten number 5 in her mouth, Lightning lowered her head and sniffed at the straw. Satisfied that all the kittens were gone, she turned around and walked out of the shed.

"Look how stiff she is," said Lulu.

"It's hard to stay still that long," Anna said.

Pam ran over to Lightning and gave her a big hug. "I'm so proud of you," she said. "You're the most wonderful pony in the world." Lightning nuzzled her shoulder like always.

Then Pam's pony galloped around the paddock. She shook her mane and whinnied as if to say, "I did a good job. Now I want to have some fun."

Snow White and Acorn ran to the fence that separated their paddock from Lightning's and whinnied at her.

Pam opened the gate that separated the two paddocks. Acorn and Snow White ran through to join Lightning in the field.

The girls laughed. "They're like us," said Lulu. "They love to have fun together."

A few minutes later Pam's parents drove up the driveway. The three girls raced to the car. They couldn't wait to tell the Crandals about Lightning's baby-sitting job.

But there was no way to tell anyone anything until the twins showed off their new shoes and the two toy horses they'd gotten for their horse collection.

Jill held out hers. "It's an Arabian," she said. "Just like the black stallion."

"Mine's a Shetland," bragged Jack. "Like Acorn."

The girls told the story of what had happened with Fat Cat and Lightning. The twins wanted to go see the kittens right away. But their parents and the Pony Pals said they should wait a couple of hours.

"If we go in too soon," Lulu told the twins, "Fat Cat might move them someplace where we won't be able to see them at all."

The twins went to their room to add the toy ponies to their collection.

"So how did Daisy do at group trail riding?" Mrs. Crandal asked Pam.

"Not too good," Pam answered. "She needs a lot of work, Mom. That pony is too easily distracted on the trail. And she's so slow. It's the opposite problem of Splash."

"I hope my new ponies aren't going to be problem ponies," Mrs. Crandal said. She sighed. "They've been a lot more work than I thought they'd be. I'm really depending on you, Pam."

"I know, Mom," Pam said.

"Did you write up about the trail ride on Daisy's training chart?" she asked.

"Not yet," Pam said.

Anna and Lulu went to the barn with Pam. Pam made the new entry on Daisy's chart.

on the trail in group	nw
comments	doesn't keep up with other ponies; easily distracted

Anna and Lulu looked at the ponies' training charts.

"I didn't know how much responsibility you had," said Lulu.

"Working two ponies every day takes a lot of time," said Anna. "You're lucky schoolwork's easy for you."

"I told my mom I wanted the job," Pam said. "And I do. But I want to be with you, too. I've got a problem."

"*You* don't have a problem," Lulu said.

"I don't?!" Pam exclaimed.

"We all have a problem," said Anna. "This is a Pony Pal Problem. So we'll all have to solve it."

Pam wasn't so sure they could solve her problem. But it was nice to know her friends were on her side.

Broken Brownies

The Pony Pals met at their school lockers the next morning.

"I've been thinking about my problem — I mean *our* problem," Pam said. "How would you two like a part-time weekend job?"

Anna and Lulu smiled at one another.

"Would this job involve schooling ponies?" Lulu asked.

"Two ponies that happen to belong to the Crandal Riding School," added Anna with a giggle.

Pam laughed. "Exactly," she said.

"It's a great idea," Lulu agreed. "If three of us work, it won't take so long."

"And we'll still have time to trail ride with our ponies," said Anna.

"Will you do it?" Pam asked. "It'd only be one hour on Saturday. And one on Sunday. And my mom said she'd pay you, too." Pam hoped with all her heart that her friends would say yes.

"It'll be good experience," said Lulu.

"It makes sense," said Anna. "If we work together we have time to ride together."

"And I could really use some help," said Pam.

"But I don't know how to train a pony," said Lulu. "Especially one that's strong-willed like Splash."

"Together we can do it," said Pam. "This Saturday we'll work on Splash and trail riding. I think we should have a lesson plan."

"Remember what Splash did last time!"

groaned Anna. "That was awful."

"This calls for three ideas," said Lulu.

"Maybe we could meet right after school," suggested Pam. "But it has to be a short meeting because I've got to get to work."

"I'm raking the yard for my grandmother after school," said Lulu. "But I could go to a meeting first." She smiled at Pam. "My grandmother pays me for yard work. I'm saving for a new saddle, too."

"Is today one of your tutor days?" Pam asked Anna. Pam knew that Anna was dyslexic and that she had a tutor twice a week to help her with reading.

"Yes," Anna answered, "but not until four o'clock."

The Pony Pals agreed to go to the Off-Main Diner for a meeting right after school.

When the Pony Pals left school that afternoon they rushed down Main Street, turned on Belgo Road, and ran over to the Off-Main Diner. Pam pulled open the big glass door. "Your mom's here," she told Anna.

Lulu sniffed the air as she walked in. "And she just made brownies."

Anna's mother owned the Off-Main Diner and was famous for her chewy chocolate brownies. The three girls took deep breaths of the warm, sweet smell of cooling brownies. They followed the smell to the counter.

Mrs. Harley looked up from cutting a huge pan of brownies. "I'm so glad you girls stopped by," she said. "I've just cut these brownies. There are some broken ones that I didn't quite know what to do with."

"We'll try to help you out, Mom," teased Anna.

The girls carried a plate of broken brownies and glasses of milk to their favorite booth in the back of the diner.

Pam opened the meeting by saying, "Our problem is how to train Splash to trail ride in a group. Lulu, go first."

"Okay," Lulu said. "Listen to this."

Don't take our ponies on the trail with Splash. For the first lesson bring just one other pony. A quiet one like Daisy.

"That's a great idea," said Pam.

"And it leads right into my idea," said Anna.

She laid a drawing on the table.

"I agree that our own ponies should all stay behind when we train the ponies," Anna said. "But Acorn, Snow White, and Lightning should all be together. That way they'll have one another and none of them will get upset when we leave."

Pam and Lulu agreed with Anna.

"My idea is about *how* to work with Splash," Pam said.

She read:

I ride Splash. Lulu walks next to Splash and directs him with a lead rope.

"That's a terrific idea," Lulu told Pam.

"I checked with my mother about it," Pam said. "She thought it was a good idea, too."

"Does your mother mind if we all work at your job on weekends?" asked Anna.

"She wonders why she didn't think of it herself," said Pam. "I just hope our plan works. Her new riding students start in two weeks."

Back on the Trail

Monday, after school, Pam worked in the ring with Splash and Daisy. Lightning watched the lesson from her paddock.

When Pam finished with the new ponies, her mother said, "I'll get the tack off these two. You go spend some time with Lightning."

Pam didn't need a lead rope to bring in her pony. The instant Lightning saw Pam coming in her direction she raced to the fence.

Every day that week, Pam worked the

new ponies. Then she took Lightning for a trail ride.

Saturday morning, Pam met Anna and Lulu as they rode off Pony Pal Trail.

"What do we do first?" Anna asked Pam.

"Go see the new kittens!" Pam answered. "Wait until you see. They're getting so cute."

After they let Acorn and Snow White out in the paddock with Lightning, the three girls ran to the barn.

They went right to the feed room and looked in the closet. Fat Cat was nursing her kittens in the cardboard box. The mother cat looked up at the three girls and purred.

"She's so proud," Anna whispered.

"Are all her babies going to be gray?" asked Lulu.

"There's one under her leg that looks like it'll be mostly white," Pam said.

"Is Fat Cat still doing mice patrol?" Anna asked.

"You bet," Pam chuckled. "She's a hard working mother *and* a mouse chaser."

"Pretty soon she'll have five helpers," said Lulu.

"We're going to give three of the kittens away," said Pam.

"So she'll have *two* helpers," Anna giggled. "Just like Pam and her *two* helpers."

"Okay, helpers," Pam said to Anna and Lulu. "Let's get to work."

With three girls saddling two ponies, Splash and Daisy were ready in a few minutes. Next, the girls led the ponies to the beginning of Pony Pal Trail.

Acorn and Snow White noticed the parade of girls and ponies. But they turned right back to grazing.

"I told you our ponies would be fine as long as they were together," Anna commented.

"Splash and I will lead," Pam said when they reached the beginning of Pony Pal Trail.

"And I'll walk next to you," Lulu said.

"Anna, make Daisy keep up with us," Pam said. "Don't let her be a slowpoke."

Splash wanted to trot or canter right away. But Pam and Lulu insisted that he keep to the walk. Splash calmed down.

"Good work, Splash," Pam said.

When it was time to move him up into the trot, Pam told Lulu, "Go back and work with Daisy. Get her to keep up with Splash."

Pam gave the direction and Splash moved right into a spirited trot. After letting him continue for awhile, Pam halted the pony. She was happy with how quickly he was responding to her. She wondered if Daisy had kept up. Pam turned in her saddle to see that the golden pony was exactly a pony length behind her. Perfect spacing for the trail!

"So far we're doing great," Pam called back to Anna and Lulu. "Now let's put Daisy first."

They turned the ponies around so Daisy would be in the lead.

"This is the hardest part of today's lesson for Splash," said Pam. "He's going to want to rush ahead."

"I'll help," Lulu said as she walked over to Splash.

Anna started Daisy off at the walk.

But Splash wanted to move right into a faster gait. When he started to trot, Pam and Lulu moved him around in a little circle. Every time Splash wanted to rush ahead, the girls moved him in another small circle.

"He'll get sick of these circles," Pam said. "Then he'll behave."

After the fifth circle, Splash finally calmed down and kept to the pace Daisy set.

"There's your mom," Lulu called back to Pam. Pam looked beyond Daisy and saw her mother walking toward them.

The three girls and two ponies stopped in front of Mrs. Crandal.

"I came out to see how it's going," she said.

Anna leaned over and patted Daisy's neck. "Daisy's doing terrific," she said.

"And Splash is staying in line a lot better," Pam reported.

"Show me," Mrs. Crandal said, "without Lulu's help. Go down to our end of the trail and back." She pointed to a big rock next to the trail. "Lulu and I will watch you from up there."

Pam was worried that Splash wouldn't do as well with people watching. But once the demonstration began she thought only about riding Splash. He worked with her better than ever.

When they completed the run, Pam brought Splash to a halt in front of the rock. "That was very good," Mrs. Crandal said. "You girls worked those ponies beautifully. You can bring them in now."

On the way home, Lulu rode Splash and Pam walked alongside the pony. After they let the new ponies out in the paddock, the Pony Pals brought their own ponies to the barn. It was time to saddle up and go for a Pony Pal trail ride.

"Now we can ride over to Mudge Road and play in that old house on the Ridley farm," Pam said.

While they tacked up their ponies, the girls talked about the house and what they'd do there. They were ready to head out on their ride when Mrs. Crandal came into the barn. Pam noticed that she was carrying three envelopes.

Mrs. Crandal handed an envelope to Anna and another to Lulu. "For your work today, girls," she said. "You did a fine job."

"Thank you," Lulu said.

"It was neat," said Anna.

"I hope I can call on you again sometime," she said.

"I thought we were working tomorrow, too," Anna said.

"That won't be necessary," Mrs. Crandal

said. She handed Pam an envelope. "This is your week's pay, dear," she said.

"Thanks, Mom," Pam said. She folded the envelope and tucked it in her back jeans pocket.

"You were a good worker, Pam," her mother told her. "It was very hard for awhile, but you stuck it out. It's a job well done and I'm proud of you."

"Is my job over?" Pam asked.

"Yes," Mrs. Crandal said. "My new students start next week, so they'll be working the ponies. I might need you to give Splash and Daisy a refresher course once in a while. But for now they'll be very satisfactory school ponies. Thanks to you."

When Pam's mother left, Pam turned to Lulu and Anna. "I'm out of a job," she said. "Do you know what that means?"

"It means you won't have to work after school," Lulu said.

"Or on weekends," added Anna.

The Pony Pals raised their hands to hit

high fives, but Anna dropped her hand before they did it. "Not having a job also means you won't be able to buy a new saddle," she said.

Pam thought about that for a second. Then she said, "I'll have enough money for it someday. Right now I'd rather be a Pony Pal with my old saddle."

The Pony Pals hit their high fives and shouted, *"All right!"* Lightning whinnied and nuzzled into Pam's shoulder.

Pam lay her head on Lightning's neck. "Today we're going for a nice long ride," she told her pony. "You, me, and our Pony Pals."

Runaway Pony

The author thanks Dr. Kent Kay for medical consultation on this story.

A special thanks to Margaret Barney of Broken Wheel Ranch for western riding lessons.

Contents

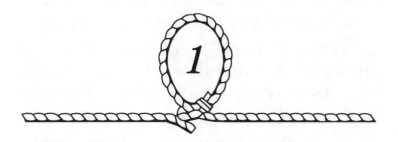

Strangles

Lulu leaned against the fence and watched her pony, Snow White, standing in the field. Snow White was sick. The beautiful pony had a stuffy nose, a bad cough, and a fever. Lulu wondered when her pony would be better.

Dr. Crandal had been treating Snow White for two weeks. He explained that Snow White had strangles, a contagious disease. Poor Snow White had to stay at the Baxters' stable where there were no other animals. Lulu felt badly that Snow White had to be separated from other ponies while she was sick. Lulu knew how much Snow White disliked being alone.

The sun was setting, and it was time to bring Snow White in for the night. "Come on, Snow White," Lulu called. "I cleaned out your stall. Let's go."

When Snow White saw Lulu coming toward her with a lead rope, she ran in the other direction. Lulu put the lead rope behind her back and held out an apple in her other hand. Snow White saw the apple and walked over to Lulu. As Snow White ate the apple, Lulu clipped the lead rope on the halter. "I'm sorry I tricked you," she said, "but it's for your own good."

Lulu led Snow White into the stable. While Lulu brushed Snow White, the pony looked through the open door to the field and whinnied. "You miss your pals, Acorn and Lightning," said Lulu. Snow White nudged Lulu on the shoulder. "I know how you feel. When I had strep throat, I couldn't see any of my friends, either."

Lulu added clean bedding to the stall,

piled hay in the hayrack, and put two handfuls of oats in the feed bucket.

While Snow White ate, Lulu read the
Pony Care Chart. Dr. Crandal had visited
Snow White that day and written on the
chart. Lulu read his entry.

FRIDAY, 10:00 AM

LUNGS CLEARING.
NO FEVER.
LAST DOSE PENICILLIN.
CAN GO HOME IN TWO DAYS.

DR. C

"Snow White," Lulu shouted happily,
"you're coming home!" Lulu added her
entry to the Pony Care Chart.

Friday, 5:30 P.M.
½ hour outdoors. More energy than
yesterday.
Did not want to come inside. Ate two
handfuls of oats.

Lulu

A horn honked. Lulu looked at her watch and knew it was Pam's mother. Mrs. Crandal was driving the Pony Pals to the movie theater in Milltown.

Lulu put on her backpack and said goodbye to Snow White. Snow White started to nicker and stomp around her stall. Snow White had never done that when Lulu was leaving her.

"I know you don't want to be alone, Snow White," Lulu said. "But you'll be coming home soon."

Snow White nickered again. Lulu wondered if she should stay with Snow White. But she really wanted to see the movie. The Pony Pals had talked about going all week. The horn honked again.

"I've got to go," Lulu told Snow White. Lulu kissed the pony on her soft cheek. "See you tomorrow," she said.

As Lulu ran across the frozen field to the car, she heard Snow White whinnying sadly. The pony seemed to be calling to Lulu, "Don't leave me."

Lulu opened the door to the Crandals' station wagon and climbed into the backseat with her friends.

"How's Snow White?" Pam and Anna asked at the same time.

"She's almost perfect again," Lulu said.

"My dad said she can come home on Sunday," said Pam.

"We're lucky the other ponies didn't catch it," Pam's mother said as she drove down Lilac Lane. "Strangles can be very serious."

"It's so great that Snow White is coming home," Anna said.

"Pretty soon we'll all be trail riding again," said Pam. "Just think, everything will be back to normal."

"I hope so," Lulu said. But all she could think about was Snow White's sad whinnies.

The Snowstorm

After the movie the Pony Pals and Mrs. Crandal went to Off-Main Diner. Anna's mother owned the diner and was working behind the counter.

Mrs. Crandal sat at the counter so that she and Mrs. Harley could talk. The girls went to their favorite booth in the back to write down what they wanted to eat. They were always their own waiter at the diner. While Lulu and Pam went behind the counter to pour their drinks, Anna went into the kitchen with their sandwich orders.

Lulu loved the way the Pony Pals worked together. Not just for simple things like getting their own food at the diner. But for big things, like solving difficult problems.

Pam and Lulu were waiting at the booth with their drinks when Anna came out of the kitchen with their sandwiches and fries. While the three friends ate, they made plans for the next day.

Anna offered to help Lulu with her morning chores for Snow White. For two weeks Lulu had been going to the Baxters' twice a day to take care of her pony. "After chores tomorrow, let's all go for a hike," suggested Anna.

"I'm training a pony for my mother's riding school at nine o'clock," Pam said. "But I can meet you at the Baxters' around ten-thirty."

"A hike sounds like fun," said Lulu. "But I'll be glad when we can all go trail riding together again." Pam and Anna agreed.

The Pony Pals loved to trail ride through the woods and fields around Wiggins. Snow

White and Anna's pony, Acorn, shared a paddock and shelter behind Anna's house. A mile-and-a-half trail, called Pony Pal Trail, connected that paddock to the Crandals' farm. Pam's pony, Lightning, lived there with many other Crandal ponies and horses.

Pam Crandal was a real horse lover and knew loads about them. She learned a lot from her dad, who was a veterinarian. Pam was a hard worker. She helped train ponies with her mom, who was a riding instructor. Pam was also the smartest person in their grade at school.

Anna Harley didn't like school very much. She was dyslexic, which meant reading and writing were hard for her. But Anna was smart, a great artist, and always full of fun.

Having good friends was especially important to Lulu. Her mother died when she was little and her dad often worked in faraway places. Anna and Pam had been friends since kindergarten. But Lulu didn't meet them until fifth grade when she moved to Wiggins to live with her grandmother.

Anna passed the plate of french fries to Lulu. "Let's have a welcome home party for Snow White," Anna said.

"We can make our ponies a special warm mash with oats, carrots, and apples," Pam said.

The Pony Pals hit high fives. A welcome home party for Snow White would be so much fun! Lulu was glad to have friends like her Pony Pals.

The next morning Lulu woke to see Wiggins covered with a thick blanket of snow. "I didn't know it was going to snow," she said to her grandmother at breakfast.

"The snow started around midnight," her grandmother said. "For a couple of hours it was blowing and coming down hard. The wind kept me awake. I'm surprised you slept through it."

There was a rap on the kitchen door and

Anna walked in. Her cheeks were red from the cold, but she was smiling. "I'm so glad we're going to be outside all day," she exclaimed.

"Me too," said Lulu.

"Brr-rr," said Grandmother Sanders. Lulu's grandmother wasn't the outdoor type. She owned a beauty parlor and cared more about looking proper than outdoor sports.

Lulu packed her backpack for the hike, put on her warmest jacket, and kissed her grandmother good-bye. Outside, the sky was blue and the wind had stopped blowing. Lulu and Anna tramped through the snow to the Baxters'.

"I love it when I'm the first one to walk in the snow," Anna said.

"Snow White does, too," said Lulu. "I can't wait to let her out in it."

The girls turned a corner in Lilac Lane and faced the Baxters' property. Lulu suddenly felt that something was wrong. As they walked closer she noticed that the paddock gate was open and blowing in the wind.

"I wonder who opened the door?" said Lulu.

"The stable door is open, too," said Anna.

The girls ran through the paddock to the stable. Snow White's stall was empty.

"Maybe she's outside and we didn't see her because she's white and the snow is white," Anna said.

Lulu and Anna ran back outside and looked all over the snowy paddock. All was quiet. They didn't see Snow White.

Lulu's pony was gone!

No Clues

"Oh, Anna," Lulu cried. "Where's Snow White?"

"Don't worry, Lulu," Anna said. "We'll find her."

"She wanted to go home with me last night," Lulu said. "Maybe that's where she went. Maybe she's in the paddock with Acorn right now."

Anna shook her head. "I would have seen her when I fed Acorn this morning," she said.

"And she wasn't on the road between our

house and here," said Lulu. "Or we would have seen her." Lulu felt like crying. But she knew tears wouldn't help find Snow White.

"When Snow White came down with strangles, we were at the Crandals'," said Lulu.

"And we came here right from there," added Anna, "so Snow White knows the way to the Crandals'."

"Maybe that's where she is," said Lulu.

Anna pointed toward Lilac Lane. "There's Pam. Let's ask her."

Anna and Lulu ran across the snowy field. The three friends met at the open gate.

"Did you see Snow White?" Anna and Lulu asked at the same time.

"No, isn't she here?" Pam asked. Her eyes were wide with surprise.

"Snow White ran away," said Anna.

"When?" asked Pam.

"She was gone when we got here," Anna answered.

"If Snow White didn't go home or to Pam's," Lulu said, "where did she go?"

"Let's look in the snow and see where her hoofprints lead," Pam suggested.

The girls looked all over the field. They didn't find one hoofprint.

"That's so strange," said Pam. "There are at least three inches of snow. How could Snow White run away and not make hoofprints?"

"Maybe she ran away while it was still snowing," said Anna. "Or maybe before it snowed."

"My grandmother told me it stopped snowing at about two in the morning," said Lulu.

"It's ten o'clock now," said Pam. "That means Snow White's been gone for at least eight hours already."

The Pony Pals looked at one another. They were all frightened for Snow White.

"Maybe she tried to go home or to Pam's," said Lulu, "and got lost because of the snowstorm." Lulu's eyes filled up with tears. Pam put an arm around Lulu's shoulders. "Don't worry," she said, "we'll find Snow White."

"What if she hurt herself in the storm?" said Lulu. Her voice trembled. "What if she broke her leg?"

"Come on, Lulu," said Anna. "Let's see if Mrs. Baxter is home. Maybe she saw Snow White."

"And let's call the state police to see if anybody's reported seeing a lost pony," Pam suggested.

"Look," Anna said, "Mrs. Baxter is getting into her car."

As the girls ran toward the car they shouted to Mrs. Baxter to wait.

"Snow White's gone," Lulu said. "Did you see her anywhere?"

"No," said Mrs. Baxter. "What happened?"

"She ran away," answered Pam.

"Oh, dear," said Mrs. Baxter. "Poor Snow White. I have real estate appointments to show houses this morning, girls. But I'll come home right after. I want to help you find Snow White."

"Thank you," said Lulu. "Could we use your phone to call the state police?"

"Of course," answered Mrs. Baxter. "The kitchen door is unlocked. And the phone number for the police station is on the list of emergency numbers next to the phone. Stay there as long as you like."

The girls went into the house. Pam dialed the number for the state police and handed the phone to Lulu.

"I would like to report a missing pony," Lulu told the police officer who answered the phone.

The police officer asked Lulu a lot of questions like, "What color is the pony?" and "How big is the pony?" Then he said, "Hold on. I'll check the computer."

Lulu looked through the Baxters' kitchen window. She could see the open stable door and the empty paddock. Oh, Snow White, she thought. Where are you?

A minute later the officer was back on the phone with Lulu. "A dog was hit by a truck on Route Forty-one during the storm," he told her. "And there are two reports of cars hitting deer. Nothing about a pony. But it's early in the day," he added. "Something might still come in."

Lulu told the officer her grandmother's phone number and hung up the Baxters' phone.

Talking to the police gave Lulu a new idea of what might have happened to Snow White. "Maybe Snow White got hit by a car," she told her friends. "And she was injured or . . ." She couldn't finish the sentence.

"I wish ponies wore identification tags, like dogs," said Pam. "Then if someone found Snow White they'd know who to call."

"Snow White's so beautiful," said Lulu. "Maybe someone found her and wants to keep her."

"That would be better than being lost or hurt," said Anna.

"I don't think Snow White would like someone who would steal a pony," said Lulu.

"Don't worry, Lulu," Pam said. "We've solved big problems before. And we'll do it again."

"But we've always had clues to follow," said Lulu. She pointed out the window to the Baxters' snowy field. "Today the snow is covering up Snow White's tracks and any other clues she might have left."

"Lulu, you've tracked animals with your dad," Anna said.

"I was just thinking about that, too," said Pam. "You're great at tracking, Lulu."

Lulu wished her father was in Wiggins instead of in Africa. Mr. Sanders studied wild animals and wrote about them. Everything Lulu knew about tracking animals she had learned from her father.

Lulu couldn't help feeling happy for a

second. She loved it when the Pony Pals all had the same idea at the same time. But the happy feeling left quickly.

"If I had stayed with Snow White in the stable last night," Lulu said, "she wouldn't have run away. It's all my fault."

The Search Begins

The Pony Pals stayed in the Baxters' kitchen while they figured out what to do next.

Anna put her hand on Lulu's shoulder.

"Lulu, it was too cold for you to sleep in the stable last night," Anna said. "It's not your fault."

"I still should have stayed," said Lulu. "I have a warm sleeping bag."

"I know you feel badly, Lulu," Pam said. "But blaming yourself isn't going to find Snow White."

Lulu knew that Pam was right. "Let's come up with three ideas about how to find her," Lulu said.

"I have an idea," said Anna. "We should make posters and put them up around town. My sister and I did that when her cat, Tabby, got lost. Someone found him and called us because they saw the poster in the grocery store."

"Posters are a good idea," said Pam.

"Especially if Snow White got lost in town," said Lulu. "But if Snow White's lost in the woods, we have to find her ourselves."

"One of us could make posters for town," said Pam, "while the other two search the woods."

"Anna, you're the best artist," said Lulu. "Will you do the posters?"

"Sure," said Anna. She pulled a piece of paper from a message pad on the Baxters' kitchen counter. Anna went right to work on an idea for a missing pony poster.

"My idea is to search for Snow White on

Mudge Road Extension," said Lulu. She took a piece of paper from the pad, too. Then she drew a map.

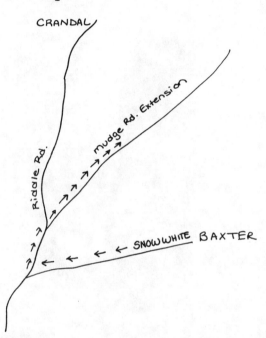

"I think Snow White was headed toward the Crandals'," explained Lulu. "Then the snowstorm started and she got lost. There aren't any roads going to the left, so Snow White probably went to the right." Lulu pointed to Mudge Road Extension. "We should look there."

"That's a good idea," said Pam.

"I wish I could make signs and search, too," said Anna.

"It's more important for you to make posters," said Lulu.

Anna showed her idea for a poster to Pam and Lulu. They helped her with spelling some of the words.

MISSING PONY

HER NAME IS SNOW WHITE

Color : white
Height : 13.2 hands (54 inches)
If found call : 555-0011

"That's perfect," said Lulu. "Making signs and putting them up is a big help, Anna."

"I'll go home and do them right away," Anna said.

While Anna was putting on her jacket, Pam told them her idea. "Lightning can help us find Snow White," she said. "Ponies have a great sense of smell."

"Aren't you afraid that she'll catch strangles?" asked Lulu.

"No," said Pam. "Finding Snow White is more important. If you were lost and had strep throat, we'd want to help find you. Even if we might catch it."

"Lightning and Acorn would feel the same way," added Anna.

"Thanks," said Lulu. "I think it's a good idea for Lightning to help. Besides, if Lightning finds Snow White, we can still keep them apart."

Anna opened the door to leave. "I'll come back here as soon as I'm finished with the signs," she told her friends. "Good luck."

After Anna left, Pam and Lulu made their plan. Pam would run home to tell her parents that Snow White was missing and to saddle up Lightning. Then Pam would ride Lightning to meet Lulu on Mudge Road. Meanwhile, Lulu would look for clues along Lilac Lane and Mudge Road. "But before I leave, I'll pack up emergency supplies and food for Snow White," Lulu said. "We'll need them . . . if we find her."

"We'll find her," Pam said. "Be sure to wait on Mudge Road for me, Lulu. Don't go into the woods alone. We have to stick together."

"I'll wait for you," promised Lulu.

Pam left the Baxters'.

Lulu already had water and an apple in her backpack. And her whistle was hanging around her neck. But there were other things she needed. Three clean dish towels were hanging on a rack. If Snow White had a bad cut, Lulu could use those towels for bandages. She knew Mrs. Baxter wouldn't mind if she borrowed them. So Lulu put them in her backpack. Next Lulu went out to the stable. She put a small bag of oats, a halter, and a lead rope in her backpack. She zipped the bag shut and ran out of the stable. She had to find her pony.

As she walked onto Lilac Lane, Lulu thought, I must have left Snow White's stall door open last night. That was how she broke out of the stable. And I didn't chain the paddock gate because I thought Snow White would be in the stable all night. I was in such a big hurry to go to the movie that I didn't take good care of my pony.

Lulu didn't bother to wipe away the tears that dropped on her cheek. She didn't care if they froze there. Her pony was lost.

Lost

Lulu walked slowly along Lilac Lane. She was looking for clues that would lead her to Snow White. But she didn't see any. She turned right off Lilac Lane and headed up Mudge Road.

Lulu noticed some tracks in the snow along the edge of the road. As she ran toward the tracks she thought, Maybe Snow White didn't go off the road until the snow stopped. Maybe those are her tracks and I can follow them until I find her. Lulu ran up to the tracks and bent to study them.

They weren't tracks that a pony's hooves would make. Coyotes made those tracks. A whole pack of coyotes. What if Snow White was injured and coyotes found her? Lulu knew that coyotes killed injured or weak deer. Why not a pony?

Lulu was sad and worried as she walked on. But she was also determined to find her pony. She wished Pam and Lightning would hurry up.

Lulu was close to the spot where Mudge Road split into Riddle Road and Mudge Road Extension. She stared into the thick woods. Was Snow White somewhere in those woods? And if she was, why didn't she find her way out when it stopped snowing? Had Snow White fallen and hurt herself? Had the coyotes already found her?

Lulu remembered her father's advice about tracking animals. "Take your time and look for details. Most clues are small."

Lulu looked into the woods as she walked along. Suddenly she spotted a strand of creamy white hair caught on the low branch of a tree.

Was it hair from Snow White's mane? Lulu walked up to the tree. She knew the hair might be from a deer. She'd often seen the white hair from their tails caught on fences and branches. Lulu took off her gloves. She pulled the hair off the branch. The strands were much longer than the hair from a deer's tail. She rubbed the strands of hair between her fingers. They were coarse and oily like Snow White's mane. "Snow White," Lulu whispered toward the woods. "Snow White, you came this way."

Lulu had promised Pam she'd stay on the road. And Lulu's father had taught her never to go in the woods alone. But Lulu couldn't wait. She had to keep searching.

There were no trails to follow. And there was so much snow that she didn't know if she'd even recognize a trail if she found one. No wonder Snow White's lost, Lulu thought.

Lulu called out Snow White's name. Then she stood still and listened for an answer. All she heard was the soft plop of snow falling off pine tree limbs. She kept walking.

Lulu was discouraged. She had no idea how to find Snow White. And now she was lost. I could find my way back to Mudge Road by following my own tracks in the snow, she thought. But I'm not going back. Snow White came into the woods. She must be somewhere around here.

Lulu was thirsty. But she didn't drink the water in her backpack. I have to save it for Snow White, she thought. She looked up and saw that the sky was darkening with clouds. What if it snowed again? Snow would cover her tracks. How would Lulu find her way back to Mudge Road then?

As she walked farther into the woods, Lulu shouted out Snow White's name. But no familiar whinny answered her call. Once, through the trees, Lulu thought she saw Snow White lying down, covered with snow. Snow White is dead, she thought. Lulu pushed through the prickly brush to get to her pony. But the lump wasn't Snow White. It was a bush weighed down by snow.

Lulu saw a stone fence behind the bush. I'm on the Ridley farm, she thought. No one had lived on the Ridley farm for over one hundred and fifty years. The main house and barns had fallen down. All that was left were piles of stones and cellar holes where the buildings used to be. Some people said the Ridley farm was haunted. Lulu didn't believe in ghosts that much. But being alone on the Ridley farm still gave her the creeps.

Lulu walked on.

Soon she spotted a mound of manure in the snow. It looked as if it had come from a pony. Lulu broke off a branch from a tree and poked through the frozen outside layer of manure. Inside, the manure was still soft. Lulu's heart beat fast. Snow White left this pile, she thought. What other pony would be in these woods during a storm?

"Snow White!" Lulu called. "Can you hear me?" She called to her pony over and over again. In between her shouts, she listened for a response.

Finally Lulu heard something. She listened carefully. It was Snow White's whinny!

"I'm coming, Snow White!" Lulu shouted. Snow White whinnied again. This time Lulu paid attention to the direction Snow White's call came from. She turned to her right and ran toward the sound.

Lulu's heart was pounding. She was excited and frightened. She found Snow White. But her pony's whinny sounded hoarse. Was Snow White's strangles worse? Was she injured? And how would Lulu get Snow White out of the woods?

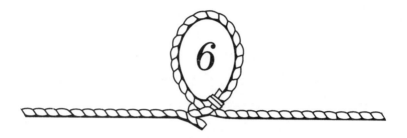

S.O.S.

Lulu ran through the cold and snowy woods toward the sound of her pony's whinny. "I'm coming!" Lulu shouted. She pushed through the bush into a clearing.

Snow White's call sounded very close now. Lulu stopped and looked around. She could hear Snow White, but she could not see her. Was that because her pony was the color of snow? Or was Snow White buried *under* snow?

Finally, Lulu realized that Snow White's whinny was coming from in the ground.

Lulu came to the edge of a hole that had been the cellar for the Ridley farmhouse. She looked down and saw . . . Snow White!

Snow White looked up and saw Lulu, too. The pony nickered happily and charged around the floor of the cellar. Lulu realized that Snow White had jumped or fallen into the hole and couldn't get out. She was relieved to see that Snow White hadn't broken any bones. The pony nickered again. She seemed to be saying, "Glad to see you, Lulu. Now get me out of here."

Lulu lay on her stomach and reached out her arm. Snow White came over to her. "Snow White," she said. "I'm so glad you're all right and that I found you." Lulu stroked Snow White's forehead. Snow White's hide felt warm. Did she have a fever again? Was her strangles worse? Lulu had to work quickly.

Snow White probably hadn't had food or water since the evening before. Lulu took her water bottle and the bag of oats out of her backpack. Lulu wondered if she should

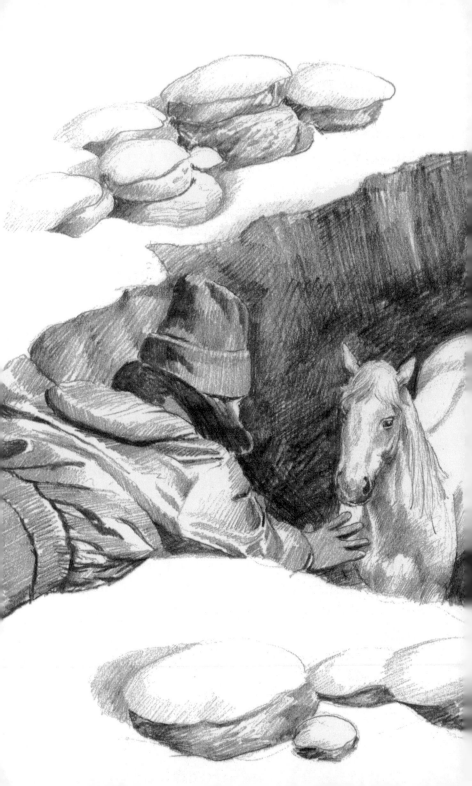

jump into the cellar hole to be with Snow White. The sides of the cellar were crumbling stone walls covered with ice and snow. If I go down there, Lulu thought, I might not be able to get out.

Lulu decided to stay where she was and leaned carefully over the cellar hole. Snow White lapped water out of Lulu's hand and ate the oats and an apple. When Snow White was finished eating, she looked up at Lulu and whinnied. Lulu knew her pony was saying, "That was good. Now get me out of here."

"Don't worry, Snow White," Lulu said. "I'll get you out." Lulu wished with all her heart that her Pony Pals were with her. She needed Pony Pal Power. Maybe Pam and Lightning were in the woods now. Lulu was about to shout out Pam's name when she remembered her whistle.

Lulu's father gave the Pony Pals whistles when they went on their first overnight camping trip. The Pony Pals all used the same signals. Their S.O.S. signal was one short blast, one long blast, and another short one. The response was one long blast and that meant someone was on the way to help. Lulu raised the red plastic whistle to her lips and blew out the S.O.S. signal. Snow White was startled by the loud noise. She charged nervously around her ice-and-snow prison.

Lulu leaned over the hole again. "Sorry, Snow White," she said. She showed Snow White the whistle and blew again. This time Lulu blew softly, so Snow White could get used to the sound. The next time she blew loudly. By then Snow White wasn't afraid of the noise anymore.

After each S.O.S. call, Lulu listened for a whistle in response. Usually Lulu loved the silence of Wiggins woods, but not today. Maybe Pam doesn't have her whistle with her like I do, thought Lulu. Or maybe she's too far away to hear mine.

Lulu squatted down at the edge of the hole to pat her pony on the head. "Don't worry, Snow White," she said. "We'll get you help." Snow White threw back her head and nickered.

Lulu smiled at her pony. She stood up to try the whistle signal once more. As she stood, Lulu lost her balance and tumbled into the eight-foot-deep hole.

Lulu scrambled to her feet. Snow White gave Lulu a nudge on the shoulder. Lulu hugged her pony. "I'm okay, Snow White," she said. "But I think we're in deep trouble now."

Lulu looked around the cellar hole. One side wasn't as steep as the other three. But it was still too steep and icy for her to climb. Snow White and Lulu were both prisoners in the freezing hole.

"What a mess we're in," Lulu said. "And it's all my fault. I didn't lock the stall door or the gate and you ran away. None of this would have happened if I'd slept in the stable last night. I'm sorry, Snow White."

Snow White nudged Lulu again. The pony knew Lulu was upset and wanted her to feel better.

"Snow White, you deserve a better owner than me," said Lulu. "Someone who isn't selfish and doesn't think a silly movie is more important than her sick pony."

Being with Snow White made Lulu feel brave again. She had to get help for her pony. She knew the sound of her whistle wouldn't be loud enough coming out of the cellar hole. Lulu needed to be higher up. And the only way to do that was to get on Snow White's back.

"Snow White," she said, "I didn't have on my backpack when I fell. So I don't have your halter and lead rope. But if I could sit on you, I'd be higher up. Then maybe Pam will hear our S.O.S."

Lulu had sat on Snow White's bare back before. But she had always had a halter and rope to hold onto. She moved Snow White over to a rock. Lulu placed her left foot on the rock and flung her right leg over her pony's side. Snow White stayed perfectly still. Lulu leaned forward, stroked Snow

White's neck, and whispered, "You're the most wonderful pony in the world."

Lulu held onto Snow White's mane with one hand and raised the whistle to her lips with the other. She blew out her S.O.S. signal and wished that someone would hear her call.

The sky was full of storm clouds. Lulu watched the gray clouds gather. She shivered. It was getting colder and darker. Lulu wondered what would happen to her and Snow White if they were in the snowy prison overnight. Would her pony survive? Would she?

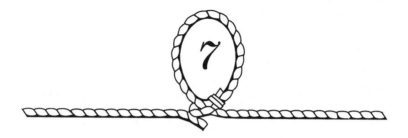

The Ice Prison

Lulu sat on Snow White's back and blew S.O.S. signals with her whistle. Suddenly, Snow White whinnied and pawed the ground. Lulu jumped off Snow White's back. As her feet hit the ground she heard a pony answer Snow White's call. She also heard Pam yelling, "Lulu, Lulu, where are you?"

"In here!" Lulu shouted back. "In a cellar hole!"

A minute later Pam and Lightning were

looking over the edge of the hole. "Lulu, are you all right?" Pam asked.

"I'm okay," answered Lulu. "But I think Snow White's strangles is worse."

"How did she get down there?" asked Pam.

"I don't know," answered Lulu. "I guess she fell in, like I did."

Pam tied Lightning's lead rope to a tree. Then she leaned over the edge of the cellar hole and put out her hand. "If you hold on to me," she said, "maybe you can climb out."

Lulu put her hands behind her back and shook her head no. "I'll stay with Snow White," she said. "If I leave she might try to follow me. She could break a leg."

"Why didn't you wait for me on the road?" Pam asked.

"Why'd you take so long?" said Lulu.

"I was looking for my parents to help us," Pam said. "My mother had gone someplace with my sister and brother. And my father is operating on a horse. I couldn't interrupt him. But I left him a note to telephone us when he finished."

"Telephone us?" exclaimed Lulu. "Here? In the woods?"

Pam patted her jacket pocket. "I borrowed his cellular phone," she said. "I don't think he'll mind. This is an emergency."

"Pam!" a girl's voice shouted. It was followed by a pony's whinny. Lulu recognized both the voice and the whinny. It was Anna and Acorn!

"Where's Lulu?" Anna asked Pam.

"Anna, I'm down here!" shouted Lulu.

Anna rode Acorn up to the edge of the hole and looked down. "You found Snow White!" she exclaimed. "Oh, Snow White, we were so worried about you."

"I'm glad you're here to help us get her out," said Lulu.

"Anna, how'd you get here so fast?" asked Pam.

"I only made one missing poster," said Anna as she dismounted Acorn. "My sis-

ter's making copies and putting signs up around town. But we don't need missing pony posters anymore. You found Snow White."

"But how did you find us?" asked Lulu.

"I followed the tracks in the snow," said Anna.

"We have to get Snow White out of here," said Lulu. "She's tired. And I think she has a fever again."

"My dad said to keep Snow White warm while she has strangles," said Pam. "It's bad for her to be out in the cold for so long."

Acorn moved closer to the edge of the cellar hole and looked at Snow White. Snow White looked back at Acorn. Anna grabbed Acorn's lead rope to keep him from going any closer to the edge.

"Anna, you'd better tie Acorn to the tree with Lightning," said Pam.

When Acorn was safely tied, the three girls talked about the problem of getting Snow White out of the hole. Pam showed

Anna the telephone. "That was a great idea," said Anna. "But I wish your dad would hurry up and call us. We could really use his help."

"Well, for now, it's up to us," said Pam. "We've got to come up with a plan. Every minute that Snow White is out here is bad for her."

"Maybe a snowmobile could drag Snow White out," said Anna. "All we'd need is some rope, a big blanket, and the snow-mobile."

"But we'd have to tranquilize Snow White first," said Pam. "Then she'd be too sleepy to walk back. And we can't drag her through the woods."

"But the snowmobile part of your idea is great, Anna," said Lulu. "What if a snow-mobile brought in some salt and sand. We could spread it on the wall to melt the ice. Then with the halter and lead rope, we could help Snow White climb out."

"We have loads of sand and salt at my

place," said Pam. "And my dad could get our neighbor Mr. Trono to drive it in with his snowmobile."

Lulu pointed at the slanted wall that wasn't as steep as the others. "If we salt and sand that wall," she said, "I bet Snow White could climb out."

Just then Lightning and Acorn snorted and whinnied in Snow White's direction.

Snow White pawed the ground and looked up as she called back to her friends.

"I'm afraid she'll try to climb out now," said Lulu. "I have a halter and lead rope in my backpack. Throw them down to me so I can hold on to her."

Lightning and Acorn snorted again. And Snow White answered. She sounded very upset.

Anna dropped the halter and lead rope into the cellar hole. But before Lulu could pick them up, Snow White began charging around the hole. Lulu couldn't bend down to get the halter and lead rope while Snow White was moving around. She had to stay clear of her pony's hooves. "Careful, Lulu," Pam warned.

Lightning and Acorn kept up their whinnies and snorts.

Snow White stomped and snorted back.

"Snow White!" Lulu yelled. "Stop. Please, stop!"

But Snow White didn't hear Lulu. She was listening to her pony friends. And she wanted to be with them. Snow White turned toward the slanted wall. She backed up. Then she snorted one more time and ran toward it.

"Oh, no!" Anna shouted. "She's going to try to climb out."

"Lulu, grab her mane!" Pam yelled.

But it was too late. Snow White was already climbing up the wall.

The wall was very steep and slippery. Snow White could easily fall and break a leg. The Pony Pals watched and held their breath.

You Can Do It!

Snow White was slipping backwards on the ice-covered rock wall. If Snow White couldn't make it out of the hole, she would crash to the cellar floor. Lulu knew only one thing the Pony Pals could do to help her. They had to cheer her on.

"You can do it, Snow White!" Lulu shouted. "I know you can."

Lightning and Acorn encouraged Snow White with loud whinnies.

"Come on, Snow White!" yelled Pam. "You're almost there."

"Go for it, Snow White!" screamed Anna.

Snow White scrambled to the top and climbed out herself. Pam and Anna cheered for her. But Snow White ignored them and ran over to her pony friends.

"Is Snow White okay?" Lulu shouted to Pam and Anna.

"There's one little cut on her shoulder," said Pam. "But it's nothing to worry about."

"Better keep her from the others," said Lulu, "because of the strangles."

But Snow White was already leaving the other ponies. She walked back over to the hole and whinnied at Lulu as if to say, "What are you still doing down there? Come on up."

"Grab her," Lulu shouted. "Before she falls back in!"

"I can't," said Pam. "She doesn't have on a halter."

"I've got pony treats in my pockets," said Anna. "I'll distract her."

Meanwhile, Lulu picked up Snow White's halter and lead rope. She tied them in a big knot and threw them up to Pam. It took three tries, but finally they landed over the top. Pam handed the halter and lead rope to Anna.

"I better get out of here myself," Lulu told Pam.

Pam lay on the snow and dropped her arm toward Lulu. But their hands didn't touch. The hole was too deep. "Wait a minute," said Pam. "I have an extra lead rope in my saddlebag."

Lulu looked up at the slippery wall Snow White had just climbed. She saw drops of blood left by Snow White's cut. Lulu thought, I'll have to be as brave as my pony.

Pam stretched out in the snow again and dropped one end of the rope to Lulu. Lulu dug her foot into the snowy rock ledge and began to take one slippery step after another.

Snow White nickered to Lulu as if to say, "Come on, you can do it."

When Lulu reached the top, she hugged her pony. They were both safe.

But Lulu was happy for only a second. Snow White felt warm against her cheek and she was panting. Was Snow White's strangles worse?

A ringing sound startled the girls and their ponies. "What's that?" Anna said.

Pam giggled. "It's the telephone," she said.

Pam took the phone out of her pocket and talked into it. "Hi, Dad," she said. Pam told her father all about the cellar hole prison; how Snow White climbed out to be with Lightning and Acorn; and how Lulu had climbed out using a lead rope.

"Let me talk to him," said Lulu. She told Dr. Crandal that Snow White was feverish and shivering.

"Bring her right into the clinic," Dr. Crandal said. "I'll check her out."

"I'm afraid Lightning and Acorn will catch strangles from Snow White," said Lulu.

"Keep them apart as best you can," he said.

Lulu said good-bye to Dr. Crandal and handed the phone back to Pam. Lulu patted Snow White on the cheek. "Sorry," she said, "you still can't be with your friends." Then she told Pam and Anna, "We have to take Snow White to the clinic."

The three girls led their ponies single file through the silent, snowy woods. Lulu and Snow White went first. After they'd gone a little way, Lulu shouted back to Pam and Anna, "You guys have saddles. You can ride home. I'll lead Snow White out following your tracks."

"I'll walk with you," said Anna.

"Me too," said Pam. "We should stick together."

As the Pony Pals walked along, Lulu could hear Pam and Anna talking about their adventure. But Lulu was quiet. She was still worried about Snow White.

When they reached the Crandals', Pam and Anna took their ponies to the barn. But Lulu went straight to the clinic with Snow White. Dr. Crandal met her at the door.

"Well, Snow White," he said, "I hear you've had quite an experience. Let's take a look at you."

Dr. Crandal smiled at Lulu and patted her on the shoulder. "You look a little worn out yourself, Lulu."

"I'm okay," said Lulu.

Dr. Crandal led Snow White into the examination room and cross-tied her. Lulu watched as he took Snow White's temperature, looked into her throat and nose, and felt her glands.

Dr. Crandal was finishing up his exam when Pam and Anna came into the room. "How is she, Dad?" asked Pam.

"She's doing all right," said Dr. Crandal. He smiled at Lulu. "Strangles isn't a problem anymore. She's just cold and tired. Since you have an open shelter at home, Lulu, it would be better if you left Snow White here overnight. A blanket, a warm mash, and a good night's sleep inside will do wonders for her."

"Can Lulu ride Snow White tomorrow?" asked Anna.

"Sure," answered Dr. Crandal. "But I'd take it easy the first time she's out. It will be a few days before she's one hundred percent again." Dr. Crandal went back into his office to meet his next patient.

"*All right!*" said Pam. "We found Snow White. And she's going to be okay."

"And we can all go trail riding together again," said Anna.

Pam and Anna raised right hands to hit high fives. But Lulu didn't raise her hand. She ran outside. She didn't want her friends to see that she was crying. Lulu knew that everything was not okay. She'd left Snow White alone and hadn't locked her stall door. She'd left the paddock gate unlocked, too. She'd almost killed her pony.

A Letter

Pam and Anna ran out to find Lulu. She was sitting on the paddock fence, crying.

"What's wrong, Lulu?" Anna asked.

"You don't understand," Lulu whispered. "It was all my fault."

"It's not your fault, Lulu," Pam said.

But Lulu just kept crying.

"I have an idea," said Pam. "Snow White's sleeping over and Acorn's already here. Let's have a Pony Pal barn sleepover tonight. There's even a heater in my mother's office."

"Then tomorrow we can go trail riding from here," said Anna.

"I can't sleep over," said Lulu. "My grandmother wants me to stay home tonight."

"When you tell her everything that's happened, I bet she'll let you sleep over," said Anna.

Lulu shook her head. "I want to go home."

Lulu saw Pam and Anna look at each other. But they didn't say any more about a sleepover.

After Lulu put Snow White in a stall in the barn, the Pony Pals went into Mrs. Crandal's office. Anna phoned her sister to tell her they'd found Snow White. Pam called Mrs. Baxter with the same good news. Meanwhile, Lulu made a warm mash for Snow White.

RECIPE FOR WARM MASH
Ingredients:

2 handfuls of oats
½ quart bran
2 cut-up apples
2 cut-up carrots

Directions:

Mix all ingredients.
Add hot tap water.
Stir well.

Anna helped Lulu make the mash. "I'll go home when you do," said Anna. "Acorn and I will walk with you. It'll be pretty on Pony Pal Trail with all the snow."

"I'm going to ask my grandmother to pick me up," said Lulu. "I'm pretty tired."

"You can ride Acorn and I'll walk," said Anna.

"My grandmother will pick me up," said Lulu. She left the office with the bowl of warm mash for Snow White.

Lulu fed Snow White and made sure her blanket was on snugly. Then she gave her pony a hug. "I love you Snow White," she said. "I'm really sorry."

Lulu stayed with Snow White until her grandmother came to pick her up. Anna and Pam followed Lulu to the car. Lulu climbed into the car beside her grandmother.

"See you tomorrow," called Pam.

"Don't forget about trail riding," added Anna.

"Bye," said Lulu.

Grandmother Sanders didn't like horses very much. But she knew Lulu did. "Tell me exactly what happened today," she said. Lulu told her everything except the scariest parts. When Lulu finished her story, Grandmother Sanders sighed. "Lucinda, you are so much like your mother. She was crazy about the outdoors and animals just like you."

Lulu's father told Lulu many stories about her mother. Her mother loved horses, too. But my mother took good care of her

horses, Lulu thought. A careless person like me doesn't deserve to have a pony.

By the time Lulu was ready for bed, she knew what she had to do. She sat at her desk, turned on the lamp, and took her stationery and a pen out of the drawer. She was ready to write a letter.

Dear Mrs. Crandal:

I want to give Snow White to you. You can use her in your riding school.

Snow White and Lightning are good friends. I know that Snow White will be very happy living at your place. I also know that you take very good care of your horses. So she will be safe, too.

Please let me know if you will take Snow White.

Sincerely Yours,
Lulu Sanders

Lulu folded the letter and put it in an envelope. Then she went to bed and cried herself to sleep.

The next morning Lulu woke up to a knock on her bedroom door. "Lucinda," Grandmother Sanders called through the door. "Anna telephoned to say it's time to go trail riding."

Lulu opened her eyes and looked at her bedside clock. It was nine o'clock. She put on her bathrobe and went down to the kitchen. Anna was knocking on the door. Lulu let her in.

"You sleepyhead!" Anna teased. "I've been up for hours. I think Acorn knows we're all going trail riding together. He's so excited. Hurry up. Get dressed."

"I'm not going with you," said Lulu. "I think Snow White should rest for another day."

"But Dr. Crandal said — "

"Besides I don't feel like riding today," added Lulu.

"But you love to trail ride," said Anna.

"I don't want to go and I don't want to talk about it," said Lulu.

Anna frowned. "If that's the way you want to be," she said.

Lulu reached into her bathrobe pocket and took out a sealed envelope. "Can you give this to Mrs. Crandal for me?" she said.

Anna took the envelope and looked at it. "What is it?" she asked.

"Just a letter," snapped Lulu.

Lulu couldn't explain. No one would understand. Not even her Pony Pals.

The Velvet Skirt

After Anna left, Lulu sat at the kitchen table and stared out into the yard. Grandmother was surprised to find her sitting there. "Aren't you riding with your friends today?" she asked.

Lulu shook her head no.

"Are you going hiking?" asked Grandmother Sanders.

"I'm going to stay indoors today," said Lulu.

"Goodness gracious," said Grandmother. "Now that's a surprise. Well, I'm going to an *indoor* brunch and an *indoor* concert with Mrs. Addison. Would you like to join us?"

"Okay," said Lulu.

A little later Grandmother met Lulu in the upstairs hall. "While you were in the shower, Pam telephoned," she said.

"Is Snow White okay?" asked Lulu.

"Pam said she's good as new. And she wanted to know what time you were coming over to go trail riding."

"Did you tell her I wasn't going?" asked Lulu.

"I told her you were going to brunch and a concert with me," answered Grandmother.

"Good," said Lulu.

Grandmother smiled. "Lucinda, dear," she said, "wear that lovely velvet skirt and the sweater with the lace collar that I bought you. You look so lovely in that outfit."

Lulu didn't care what she did or what she wore. So she put on the outfit. She even let

Grandmother fix her hair with a big lacy ribbon.

Off-Main Diner was always crowded for Sunday brunch. But Mrs. Harley made sure there was a table for her neighbors. She led them to the Pony Pals' favorite booth in the back of the diner.

"Lulu, I thought you were riding with Anna and Pam today," said Mrs. Harley.

"I'm resting today," Lulu told her.

During brunch Lulu only half-listened to Mrs. Addison and Grandmother's conversation. And she only half-ate her French toast. Her mind was on Snow White. She wondered if Snow White would miss her. Maybe she'll miss me a little bit at first, thought Lulu. But she'll be with Lightning and familiar people. And she'll be safe.

Grandmother, Mrs. Addison, and Lulu were ready to leave when Pam and Anna came running into the diner. They ran right over to the booth.

"I thought you guys were going trail riding today," said Lulu.

"We have a Pony Pal Problem to solve today," said Anna.

"We've already had one meeting," added Pam.

Lulu knew that she was the Pony Pal Problem and that the meeting had been about her. She wondered if her friends understood that she wasn't going to be a Pony Pal anymore. That she didn't deserve to be a Pony Pal.

"We're having another meeting now," said Anna. "And you have to stay for it."

"I'm going to a concert," said Lulu.

"Lulu Sanders, this is the most important meeting we've ever had," said Pam.

"Can't we have the meeting after school tomorrow?" said Lulu.

"*No!*" said Pam and Anna in unison. They said it so loudly that everyone in the diner looked at them.

"Lucinda, I think you should stay for the meeting," said Grandmother. "You haven't been yourself today. Maybe your friends can help you out of your bad mood."

After Grandmother Sanders and Mrs. Addison left, the Pony Pals settled down for their meeting.

"Do you know what our meeting was about this morning?" asked Pam.

"About my giving Snow White away to your mother," said Lulu.

"Why do you want to give Snow White away?" asked Anna.

"Anna, you know why," said Lulu. "Snow White wouldn't have been lost if it weren't for me. It was all my fault. I don't deserve to have a pony. I've made up my mind and nothing you say is going to change it."

Lulu stood up to go. "If Pam's mother won't take Snow White," she said, "I'll ask Mr. Olson to sell her through his horse farm."

Anna grabbed Lulu's skirt. "You can't go," she said. "You have to stay and hear our ideas about this problem."

"Let go of me," said Lulu. She pulled to get away from Anna. But Anna held on tight. The Pony Pals all heard the ripping sound the skirt made as it tore away from the waist.

"You better sit down," said Pam. "Before your skirt comes all the way off."

11

2 Ideas + 1

Lulu sat back down.

Pam handed her a slip of paper. "Read my solution to our Lulu problem," said Pam. "Read it out loud."

"Read it yourself," said Lulu angrily.

Lulu, it's not your fault that Snow White got out. You didn't leave the door open. Snow White broke the lock.

"How do you know the lock broke?" asked Lulu. "You just made that up."

"I did not," said Pam. "I wouldn't lie."

"Pam and I were just over there and looked at it ourselves," said Anna. "We saw that the lock was ripped right out of the wood."

"We can show you if you still don't believe us," said Pam. "Mrs. Baxter said the wood must have been rotten. She feels awful about it."

"And even if you did leave the stall door unlocked," said Anna, "that's no reason to give up Snow White. Everybody makes mistakes."

"But I knew she was lonely that night and I didn't stay with her," said Lulu sadly.

"So what?" said Pam. "Everybody gets lonely sometimes. Even ponies. You're making a big deal out of nothing. My mother thinks so, too."

"Now look at my idea," said Anna.

FRIENDS 4-EVER

Lulu looked at the drawing. She wasn't angry anymore. Her friends were right. She shouldn't give up Snow White. But she didn't let Pam and Anna know she agreed with them yet.

"Something is still wrong," Lulu said.

"What?" asked Pam and Anna.

"Whenever we solve problems we come up with three ideas, not two. So I have to have an idea. It's my turn." Lulu turned Pam's paper over and wrote on it. Then she put the paper in the middle of the table. The Pony Pals read Lulu's idea out loud.

"I'm sorry I didn't wait for Pam before we searched for Snow White," said Lulu. "I shouldn't have gone alone."

"If my pony had run away," said Pam, "I might have done the same thing."

"Me, too," said Anna.

"But we all have to remember that we work best when we work together," said Pam.

"Lulu, you had us really scared," said Anna. "I was so afraid you wouldn't understand. You can be very stubborn."

"I didn't feel like a Pony Pal anymore," said Lulu. "It's an awful feeling."

"You don't look like one either with that bow in your hair," said Anna with a giggle.

"And that fancy outfit," added Pam.

Lulu glanced at her own reflection in the diner window and laughed. "I see what you mean," she said.

"There's still time for our trail ride," said Pam. "Come on. Let's go."

"I can't leave this booth," said Lulu. "My skirt's ripped."

Anna got safety pins from the kitchen and pinned Lulu's skirt back together. Then the Pony Pals put on their jackets and left the diner.

When Lulu came out the front door she saw that their three ponies were tied to the diner's hitching post.

"Snow White!" Lulu shouted. "How did you get here?"

Snow White looked up and whinnied happily at Lulu.

"We rode over and ponied Snow White behind us on the lead rope," said Pam.

Lulu ran to Snow White and gave her a big hug. "How could I even have thought of giving you away?" she said.

"We better go over to your place so you can change," said Pam. "You can't ride in a skirt."

"Oh, yes I can," said Lulu. "My shoes have heels. And I bet you brought my helmet."

Pam laughed as she opened her backpack. She pulled out Lulu's helmet and handed it to her.

The three girls put on their helmets and untied their ponies from the hitching post.

Lulu placed her left foot in the stirrup and swung up on Snow White. *"All right!"* she shouted. The Pony Pals moved their ponies close together and hit high fives.

The ponies whinnied happily. Lulu turned Snow White toward the road. She knew she looked strange horseback riding in a skirt and her best shoes. But she didn't care. She was riding Snow White again.

Good-bye Pony

Thank you to Maria Genovesi and Dr. Kent Kay for sharing their knowledge of horses with me.

Contents

The Driving Lesson

Anna Harley sat in the cart behind her pony, Acorn. She was holding Acorn with extra-long reins called lines. Ms. Wiggins sat in the cart next to Anna. Acorn and Anna were learning carriage driving from Ms. Wiggins.

Ms. Wiggins' old pony, Winston, was watching the driving lesson from the paddock next to the Wiggins riding ring.

Anna was getting used to holding Acorn by the lines instead of shorter reins. Giving directions to a pony from a carriage was very different from giving directions from a saddle. From her seat, Anna lightly tapped Acorn's side with the whip instead of using her legs to make her pony walk on.

"Walk on," she called to Acorn. And he did.

Anna signaled with the lines and a flick of the whip for Acorn to turn left at the corner of the riding ring. Acorn made the turn then stopped in his tracks.

"Walk on," Anna called to her pony. Instead of moving forward, Acorn took two steps backward.

"Because of the blinders, he can't see Winston," Anna told Ms. Wiggins.

Anna and Ms. Wiggins had noticed that as long as Acorn could see Winston, he followed their directions. But when he couldn't see Winston, Acorn would stop suddenly and refuse to go on.

"Acorn has a mind of his own," said Ms. Wiggins.

Anna knew that Acorn could be stubborn. But Anna could be stubborn, too. And

she was determined that Acorn would be a good driving pony. Anna signaled the turn again. "Walk on," Anna commanded. Acorn walked forward.

"Good for you, Anna," said Ms. Wiggins.

Anna drove Acorn around the ring three more times. Acorn continued to act stubborn, but so did Anna.

"You are both doing very well with your driving lessons," said Ms. Wiggins. "By next winter, you and Acorn can drive in the Winter Festival parade."

Winston, put his head over the fence and nickered.

Ms. Wiggins and Anna laughed.

"Winston wants Acorn to be in the parade, too," said Ms. Wiggins.

"Acorn and Winston are great friends," said Anna.

"That's because they're both Shetland ponies," said Ms. Wiggins.

"And because Winston is so wonderful," added Anna.

"This will be the twenty-fifth year Win-

ston has led the Winter Festival parade,"
Ms. Wiggins said. "I think it's time for a
younger pony to take over."

"Acorn and I don't want to be in the parade unless you and Winston are in it, too,"
said Anna.

"Then we'll just have two pony carts lead
off the parade next year," said Ms. Wiggins.

Suddenly Acorn nickered and moved into
a trot. "Whoa!" Anna ordered. She pulled
on the lines. But Acorn trotted on.

Ms. Wiggins took the lines from Anna.
"Halt," Ms. Wiggins ordered Acorn. Acorn
obeyed Ms. Wiggins' command.

In the distance, Anna saw her friends,
Pam and Lulu, riding their ponies toward
them.

"He saw Lightning and Snow White,"
said Anna. "That's why he ran off like
that."

"Acorn's going to need a lot of work," said
Ms. Wiggins. "It's a good thing we didn't
enter him in the parade *this* year."

Ms. Wiggins and Anna were unhitching

Acorn from the cart when Pam and Lulu rode up.

"How was your lesson?" Pam asked Anna.

"Okay," said Anna. "Driving is fun. But Acorn was acting stubborn."

"As usual," teased Lulu.

Pam and Lulu tied their ponies' lead ropes to rings on the paddock fence.

Ms. Wiggins led Winston over to the driving cart. "I'm taking Winston for a drive," she said. "Anna, why don't you help me hook him up? It'll be good practice for you."

Anna helped Ms. Wiggins while Pam and Lulu saddled up Acorn. After Ms. Wiggins put on Winston's bridle, she gave him a kiss on the cheek. "My sweet, old pony," she said.

"Shetland ponies live a long, long time, right?" Anna asked.

"Yes, they do. But Winston's already thirty years old," Ms. Wiggins said. She patted Winston on the shoulder and adjusted his bridle. Then she turned to the

Pony Pals. "I have a favor to ask you girls," she said.

"What?" they said together. The Pony Pals were happy if they could do a favor for Ms. Wiggins. She was always doing nice things for them. She let them ride on the trails of the Wiggins estate anytime they wanted.

"I'll be away for a week," said Ms. Wiggins. "I'm leaving for Boston tomorrow — for an art exhibit."

"Will your paintings be in the exhibit?" asked Anna.

Ms. Wiggins smiled. "Yes," she said. "Two of my big landscape paintings. Anyway, Mr. and Mrs. Silver will be taking care of things here while I'm gone. They'll do the chores for Winston and my horse, Picasso. But when you're trail riding around here, could you visit Picasso and Winston? They really enjoy being around you and your ponies."

"Sure," said Pam.

"We'll have a Pony Party with Winston and Picasso," added Anna.

The Pony Pals mounted their ponies for the trail ride home. And Ms. Wiggins climbed into the cart.

After they all said good-bye, the Pony Pals headed east toward the trails that led home. Ms. Wiggins directed Winston toward the hills to the west. Anna turned in her saddle and watched Ms. Wiggins's cart rolling along the trail.

Lulu called back to Anna, "You coming?"

Anna squeezed her legs to tell Acorn to walk on. They soon caught up to Lulu and Pam.

"I'm going to keep Acorn forever," Anna told her friends. "I'll drive him in a cart like Ms. Wiggins drives Winston. That way I'll never outgrow him. Ms. Wiggins said that by next year we'll be good enough to drive in the Winter Festival parade with her and Winston."

The Pony Pals pulled their ponies close together and raised their right hands. They hit high fives and cheered, "All right!"

Where's Winston?

The next morning Anna and Lulu did chores together for their ponies. Anna showed Lulu the bridle with blinkers, harness, and long lines that Ms. Wiggins had lent her. "I'm going to practice with Acorn at home all this week," Anna told Lulu.

"Can I help?" asked Lulu.

"Sure. You can help me ground drive around the paddock," said Anna. "If you walk in front of Acorn, it will be a big help."

"What's 'ground drive'?" asked Lulu.

"You walk behind your pony, holding on

to the long driving lines," said Anna. "You can do it, too."

"That'll be fun," said Lulu.

Anna and Lulu caught their ponies, brushed them, and saddled them up. They were meeting Pam and Lightning on Pony Pal Trail. The trail was a mile-and-a-half and cut through the woods separating Pam's house from Anna's and Lulu's. Pony Pal Trail also led to the many trails on Ms. Wiggins' estate.

Pam and Lightning were waiting for Anna and Lulu at the three birch trees in the middle of Pony Pal Trail. Anna halted Acorn next to Pam and Lightning. "I love winter vacation," Anna told Pam. "No school for a whole week!"

"Yeah," said Pam, "it's great."

Vacations were fun for all the Pony Pals — but Anna liked them best. Anna was dyslexic. So reading and math were difficult for her. What Anna loved was drawing, painting, horses, and vacation from school. Pam and Lulu liked school a lot better than Anna did.

Pam Crandal was a terrific student and an excellent reader. She loved horses, too. Her father was a veterinarian and her mother was a riding teacher. Pam couldn't remember a time when she didn't have a pony of her own.

"I can't wait until the Winter Festival on Saturday," said Pam. "You'll love it, Lulu. It's so much fun."

This was Lulu Sanders' first winter in Wiggins, so she had never been to the Winter Festival. Lulu's father studied wild animals and wrote about them. Lulu's mother died when she was little, so Lulu lived wherever her father was working. Recently Mr. Sanders decided that Lulu should live in one place for a while. So Lulu moved in with her grandmother.

Anna knew that Lulu missed her dad. But she loved that Lulu lived right next door to her and that their ponies shared a paddock.

The Pony Pals rode side by side across a large field. "Lulu, the Winter Festival has lots of neat things," said Pam. "First, there's the parade with bands, floats, and fire trucks from the towns around here."

"And my mother sets up a food tent," said Anna. "She sells hamburgers and hot dogs. She has hot drinks and brownies, too." Mrs. Harley owned the Off-Main Diner. Everyone in Wiggins loved her food, especially her famous brownies.

"There's a big crafts fair in Town Hall," Pam said.

"And a dance at night," added Anna. "Everybody goes. Even kids."

"It sounds great," said Lulu. "I can't wait."

When they reached the other end of the field, Anna said, "Let's go visit Winston and Picasso."

"Our ponies can rest and hang out with them," said Lulu.

"We can eat our lunches there," Pam added. "Let's go!"

Anna leaned over and patted Acorn on the neck. "We're going to see your old pal, Winston," she said.

The Pony Pals galloped the whole way to the Wiggins barn and paddocks before slowing to a walk. Picasso trotted over to the fence to greet them.

"Where's Winston?" Pam asked.

Acorn nickered as if to say, "Hey, Winston, I'm here. Where are you?" But Winston didn't trot over to them the way he usually did.

"Maybe the Silvers left him in the barn today," said Lulu.

"Why would they do that?" asked Anna. "They know Winston likes to be outside."

"Let's tie up our ponies and go look for him," said Pam.

Anna clipped on Acorn's lead rope and tied him to the fence. "I'll be right back to let you out in the paddock," she told him.

The girls climbed through the fence. When Anna was a few feet into the field, she noticed a pony on the ground in the far corner. She'd never seen Winston lying down, but she knew it must be him. She pointed and shouted, "There he is."

Anna ran across the field. Her heart beat faster and faster. Is Winston sick? she wondered. Is he injured?

Help!

Anna was running so fast her feet hardly touched the ground. Pam and Lulu were running toward Winston, too. But Anna was the first to reach the old gray pony.

Anna fell to her knees by Winston's side. He raised his head, looked up at her with sad eyes, and laid his head back down.

"Oh, Winston," Anna said. "What's wrong?"

Pam walked slowly around Winston. "It doesn't look like he broke any bones," she said. "But we can't be sure."

"Maybe he's sick with colic or something," said Lulu.

"We've got to do something," Anna said.

"This is a job for a veterinarian," said Pam. "I'll go to the house and call my dad."

"And I'll go to the barn and get a halter and lead rope," said Lulu. "If he gets up, we can take him to the barn."

"Look for the Silvers, too," said Anna. "Maybe they'll know what's wrong with Winston. I'll stay here."

While her friends were gone, Anna stroked Winston's neck and talked to him. She told him that he was a wonderful pony. Winston looked up at Anna. "Don't worry, Winston," she said. "We'll take care of you."

Winston rolled over so his feet were under him.

Lulu came back from the barn. "He wants to get up," Anna told her. "Give me the halter and lead rope."

Anna put the halter on Winston's head and attached the lead rope. "Come on, Winston," she said. She pulled on the rope.

"Stand up. You can do it." Winston struggled to stand. He was wobbly on his feet, but he was up.

Pam ran over to the two girls and the pony. "Winston, you're standing!" she said. "That's a good sign."

"Did you reach your dad?" asked Lulu.

Pam nodded. "He's on his way."

"I couldn't find the Silvers," Lulu said.

"Me either," said Pam. "They must have gone shopping or something."

"Let's see if Winston will walk to the barn," said Pam. "It's the best place for my dad to take care of him."

Anna stood in front of Winston. "Come on, Winston," she said. Winston took a step forward. And then another. And another.

Suddenly Winston stopped in his tracks. Anna was afraid he was going to lie down again. She pulled at the lead rope. "Come on, Winston," she said. "You're almost there."

Lulu gave Winston a little push.

"You can do it," said Pam.

Acorn saw Winston. He whinnied loudly. Winston looked in Acorn's direction, gave a low nicker, and walked on. Anna knew he was doing it for Acorn.

When Anna finally led Winston into his stall, he lay down with a thud.

"It was hard for him to walk," said Lulu.

"He was fine yesterday," said Anna. "What could be wrong?"

"It's my job to figure that out," said a man's voice.

"Dad!" said Pam. "You're here."

"Hi, girls," said Dr. Crandal.

Dr. Crandal squatted near Winston. "Well, old pony," he said. "Let's take a look at you."

The girls leaned over the stall door and watched Dr. Crandal examine Winston. First, he listened to Winston's heartbeat with a big stethoscope. Then he felt all the bones in his legs. Dr. Crandal talked to the pony as he checked inside his ears, nostrils, and mouth.

While Dr. Crandal was examining Winston, Mr. and Mrs. Silver came into the barn. "Goodness, goodness," Mr. Silver exclaimed. "What's going on?"

The girls told the Silvers everything that had happened. Mr. Silver leaned over the stall door and looked down at Winston. "Oh, my," he said. "I remember this pony when Ms. Wiggins first got him. What a lively little fellow he was." Mrs. Silver smiled at Anna. "Just like your Acorn."

"Ah, poor old pony," said Mr. Silver. "Has his time come, Doc?"

"I think so," said Dr. Crandal. "There's not much I can do for him."

Anna went over to Dr. Crandal and looked up at him. "Aren't you going to give him medicine and make him better?" she asked.

"We'll give him something for the congestion in his lungs," said Dr. Crandal. "But the best thing we can do for Winston is make sure he's comfortable and doesn't suffer. I wish I could talk to Ms. Wiggins."

"I have a phone number for her in Boston.

She's staying with friends," said Mr. Silver. "I'll go up to the house and write it out for you."

"What else can we do for him?" asked Anna.

"You can keep him warm," said Dr. Crandal. "And make him a warm mash. But don't worry if he doesn't eat it."

"He has to eat if he's going to get better," said Anna. "And shouldn't he stand up?" she asked.

"Let him rest for now," said Dr. Crandal. "But if he stands up later that'd be good. It's a bad sign when an old pony won't get up."

"I want to stay with him tonight," said Anna. "Ms. Wiggins would want me to."

"We could all stay here," said Lulu. "And have turns taking care of Winston."

"Can we, Dad?" asked Pam.

Dr. Crandal thought about it for a few seconds. "What do you two think?" he asked Mr. and Mrs. Silver. "Could you put up with these gals tonight?"

"If Ms. Wiggins were here she'd be up all night with Winston herself," said Mr. Silver. "She loves that pony."

"And we have plenty of beds," added Mrs. Silver.

"Could we sleep in the barn?" asked Pam. "That's what we usually do for sleepovers."

"The tack room is heated," said Mr. Silver. "I suppose you could."

Anna knew that if Pam had permission to stay over, she'd get permission, too.

"My grandmother will let me stay if you both can," said Lulu.

Acorn whinnied loudly. He seemed to be saying, "What's going on in there? Where's my pal, Winston?"

Anna had an idea. "Dr. Crandal, can Acorn stay in the stall next to Winston tonight?" she asked. "They're very good friends."

"I don't see why not," said Dr. Crandal.

Before Dr. Crandal left, he told the girls and the Silvers to telephone him if Winston's condition changed.

Anna went out to the barn to get Acorn. She gave him a hug. "Winston is very sick," she said. Acorn nickered and nuzzled into Anna's shoulder. "Don't worry, Acorn," she said. "We'll make Winston better. The Pony Pals have solved tough problems before. And we'll solve this one."

Night Watch

The Pony Pals took care of Winston all day. At dinnertime, Mr. Silver came into the barn. "You girls go up to the house and eat your supper," he said. "I'll stay with Winston."

Mrs. Silver had made them spaghetti, salad, and apple pie. When they finished eating, Pam and Lulu stayed to help with the dishes. Anna went back to the barn to take Mr. Silver's place. She was disappointed to see Winston still lying down.

"Did he eat anything?" Anna asked.

Mr. Silver shook his head. "He's just been lying there," he said. "Doc Crandal stopped to check on him and drop off your sleeping bags. I put them in the tack room."

"What did he say about Winston?"

"Just to call him if there's a change, Anna," said Mr. Silver. He shook his head sadly. "It doesn't seem like Winston's ever going to get up again."

When Lulu and Pam came back to the barn, the Pony Pals made out a chart with a schedule for their night's watch.

	Food	Water	Standing
8-10 Pam			
10-12 Lulu			
12-2 Anna			
2-4 Pam			
4-6 Mr. Silver			
6-8 Lulu			
8-10 Anna			

Wake others and phone Dr. C. If Winston seems to be suffering.

At eight o'clock, Pam began her watch. Anna and Lulu went to the tack room. They laid out their sleeping bags and slipped into them. They fell asleep talking about Winston.

"Anna, wake up." Anna opened her eyes. Lulu was leaning over her. "It's your turn," she said.

Anna unzipped her sleeping bag. She still had on her clothes. She put on her boots and splashed cold water on her face. Lulu handed her a container of apple juice and a box of cookies.

"Did Winston stand up?" Anna asked Lulu.

"He's been sleeping lying down," said Lulu. "He slept the whole time." Lulu was already snuggled up in her sleeping bag. "Good night," she said.

Anna left the tack room and went to the horse stalls. Acorn was sleeping on his feet — as usual. Anna looked at Winston lying in the straw. She remembered what Mr. Silver said: "It doesn't look like the old pony will ever get up again."

Anna went into the stall and sat next to Winston. She felt like crying. Poor Winston! He acted so sick. How come no one was trying to save his life? How could they just let him die?

Anna thought Ms. Wiggins wouldn't give up on Winston. Everything would be different if Ms. Wiggins were here. Ms. Wiggins had trusted the Pony Pals to watch out for Winston. Anna had to do something.

Acorn woke up and nickered softly. He could see Anna through the bars that separated the stalls. "Acorn," Anna said, "we're not going to let Winston die." She scratched Winston's head through the thick mane. "Wake up, Winston," she said. "Time to stand up."

First Anna tried bribing Winston with a carrot. He wasn't interested. Next, she tried pushing him. No luck. She put on his halter and lead rope and tried pulling him upright. But Winston didn't budge. He looked up at Anna and gave a weak whinny as if to say, "Leave me alone."

But Anna didn't give up. "Get up, Winston," she said. "You have to." Winston suddenly rolled onto his legs and slowly stood up. "You did it, Winston!" Anna said excitedly.

Acorn nickered at Winston. The old pony looked back at Acorn. But he was too sick and too tired to make any sound.

"Now it's time to eat," said Anna. She held the mash out to Winston. But he didn't want it. "Do you want water first?" asked Anna. He didn't want water, either. "Well at least you're standing," Anna told him.

At two o'clock Anna was supposed to wake up Pam. But she didn't want to leave Winston alone, even for a minute. She was afraid he'd lie down again.

Around two-thirty, Pam came to take her turn. "Why didn't you wake me up?" she asked Anna.

"Look," Anna said. She pointed to Winston.

"He's standing!" said Pam.

"If he's standing he can get better," said Anna. "I know he can. Try to get him to drink and eat during your watch. And don't let him lie down. He can sleep standing up, just the way he always did."

"It's great that he's standing," said Pam. She stroked the old pony's cheek. "Good for you, Winston."

Anna went back to the tack room to sleep. She needed her rest. Tomorrow she was going to be taking care of Winston. Tomorrow she was going to make Winston better. She crawled into her sleeping bag and fell asleep.

Anna woke up suddenly. Where was she? She looked around and saw that she was in Ms. Wiggins' barn. And she remembered that Winston was sick. She unzipped her sleeping bag and pulled on her boots. Pam's and Lulu's sleeping bags were empty. Anna glanced at her watch. Eight-thirty. She'd overslept.

Anna ran out of the tack room toward Winston's stall. Lulu and Pam were standing in the aisle of the barn talking.

Lulu saw Anna first. "Hi, sleepyhead," she said. "We cleaned Acorn's stall and fed him for you."

"Where's Winston?" asked Anna. Before they could answer, Anna saw where Winston was. He was lying on the floor of his stall. "How come he's lying down?" she said. "What happened?"

"He went down about halfway through my turn," said Pam.

"You were supposed to keep him on his feet," said Anna. She was angry. "It was important," she shouted.

Acorn nickered as if to say, "What's wrong?" Winston opened his eyes, looked at Anna, and shut them again.

Mr. Silver came into the barn. "Breakfast is ready, girls," he said. "I'll stay with Winston."

"I'm not hungry," said Anna. "I'll stay here." She turned her back on Pam and Lulu.

Lulu put a hand on Anna's shoulder. "It's not Pam's fault that Winston went back down," said Lulu.

"There's nothing more we can do for Winston," said Pam.

Anna glared at Pam and Lulu. What was *wrong* with her friends? The Pony Pals never gave up on a problem. "I'm not giving up," she said.

The Phone Call

Pam and Lulu went up to the house for breakfast. But Anna stayed with Winston. She put his halter and lead rope back on him. "Come on, Winston," she said. "It's time to stand up. You can do it." She gave a little pull on the lead rope. Winston didn't budge.

"Let him be, Anna," a man's voice said. Anna looked up. It was Dr. Crandal.

"He stood up last night," Anna said. "For about two hours."

Dr. Crandal looked at the chart the girls

had made. "I see," he said. "But he didn't have any food or water. Let's take a look at you, Winston."

Anna left the stall while Dr. Crandal examined Winston. Anna leaned over the gate and watched. "What's wrong with him?" she asked. "What disease does he have?"

"Winston doesn't have a disease," said Dr. Crandal. "He's dying of old age. All his systems are giving out. His heart, his lungs, his digestive system."

"Can't you fix them?" Anna said.

Dr. Crandal shook his head. "Sometimes you just have to let nature take its course, Anna," he said.

Mr. Silver came into the barn and stood beside Anna. "What do you think, Doc?" he asked.

"Same thing as I thought last night," said Dr. Crandal. "Winston is dying. I'd like to put him out with an injection tonight."

"Ms. Wiggins wouldn't want him to suffer," said Mr. Silver. "That's a fact."

"I haven't been able to reach her," Dr. Crandal said. "I want to talk to her before I put him down."

"She knew Winston might not make it through the winter," said Mr. Silver. "I dug a hole before the ground froze, just in case."

Dr. Crandal and Mr. Silver were talking about putting Winston to sleep forever. Anna didn't know what to say or do. *Everyone* was giving up on Winston.

Pam and Lulu came into the barn. "Anna, Mrs. Silver said to go up to the house for pancakes," said Pam.

"She makes great blueberry pancakes," said Lulu.

"I'm not hungry," said Anna. How could Pam and Lulu think of food now?

Pam went into the stall and stood by her father. "Morning, honey," he said.

"Hi, Dad. How's Winston?" Pam asked.

"It's time to say good-bye to Winston," Dr. Crandal answered.

"We'll stay with him, Dad," said Pam quietly.

"I'll stop by between my other barn calls," Dr. Crandal said.

"Isn't there something we can do to make him better?" asked Lulu.

"He won't get better," said Dr. Crandal. "Just keep him comfortable."

"What if he stands up again?" asked Anna.

"I don't think he will," said Dr. Crandal. "He hasn't the strength." Dr. Crandal went up to the house to telephone Ms. Wiggins in Boston.

The Pony Pals were alone with Winston. "Poor old pony," said Pam. "We'll miss you." Pam was crying.

"Ms. Wiggins is going to feel so bad she wasn't here," said Lulu. She was crying too.

Anna wasn't crying. She was too angry to cry. "Why are you giving up on Winston?" she asked. "We're the Pony Pals. We're supposed to solve problems."

"I saw a horse die of old age once," said Pam. "He acted just like Winston."

"And Dr. Crandal said there's no hope," said Lulu. "He should know."

Anna thought, Dr. Crandal is the problem. We need to find another veterinarian. One who would try to save Winston's life instead of killing him. Dr. Crandal was Pam's father. So Anna didn't tell Pam her idea. She needed to talk to Ms. Wiggins. "I'm going up to the house," she told Pam and Lulu.

"We'll stay here with Winston," said Pam.

Anna ran all the way to the house. Dr. Crandal was talking on the phone. "Okay," he said into the phone. "I'll call you when it's over." Anna knew he was talking to Ms. Wiggins.

"I want to talk to Ms. Wiggins, too," Anna told Dr. Crandal.

"Hold on," Dr. Crandal said into the phone. "Anna Harley wants to talk to you. This is pretty rough on the girls."

Anna took the phone. She was glad that Dr. Crandal left right away.

"Hi," she said to Ms. Wiggins.

"Hello, Anna," Ms. Wiggins said back. "I

hear my poor old Winston is dying." Anna could tell Ms. Wiggins was crying.

"Winston can't die," said Anna.

"Dr. Crandal says he's dying," said Ms. Wiggins.

"Winston stood up for me last night," Anna said. "Dr. Crandal doesn't even try to make him stand up. He's given up on Winston. I think we should get another doctor."

"Anna, I trust Dr. Crandal," said Ms. Wiggins.

"Please," said Anna. "My mother will help me find another doctor. I know Winston can get better. I just know it."

"Anna, I'm sorry that I'm not there," Ms. Wiggins said. "Maybe then I could help you understand. Winston's had a long, wonderful life. I want him to die peacefully. It's time to say good-bye to Winston. Will you say good-bye for me?"

"Aren't you coming home?" asked Anna.

"I might not make it in time," said Ms. Wiggins.

Anna was shocked. Ms. Wiggins wouldn't let her get another veterinarian. And she wasn't even going to be there to say good-bye to Winston herself.

As Anna was hanging up the phone, Pam came running into the hall. "Winston is standing up!" she shouted. "Hurry, Anna."

Anna ran back to the barn with Pam. She thought, maybe *I'm* right and everyone else is wrong. Maybe we can still save Winston's life.

Bad Pony!

Anna and Pam ran into the barn. Pam pointed toward the stalls. "Look," she said.

Anna saw that Winston was standing. His head reached over the stall door. Acorn's head was hanging over his door, too. Winston and Acorn were looking at one another and rubbing noses. Lulu stood nearby. She smiled at Anna. Pam and Anna walked quietly toward Lulu and the ponies.

"How did you get Winston to stand up?" asked Anna.

"We didn't do it," said Lulu. "Acorn did."

"He nickered at Winston until he got up," Pam said.

"Acorn," Anna said, "you're a great nurse and friend."

Acorn didn't look at Anna. All of his attention was on Winston.

"I'm going to put Winston's lead rope back on," said Anna. "So we can keep him standing. Lulu, will you make him a fresh warm mash? Maybe he'll finally eat something."

Suddenly, Anna saw Acorn give Winston a little push with his nozzle.

"Acorn, don't!" said Anna. "Don't push him!"

But it was too late. Winston took a wobbly step backward and lay down in a heap on the straw.

"You're a bad pony, Acorn," Anna scolded. "Why did you do that?"

Acorn ignored Anna. He turned in his stall and looked down at Winston through the bars.

"Don't scold Acorn," Pam told Anna. "He didn't do anything wrong."

Anna opened the door to Acorn's stall and went in. "He pushed Winston over," she said angrily.

"I think he was just telling Winston that it is okay to die," said Lulu.

"And saying good-bye," added Pam.

Anna didn't care what her friends thought. She slipped on Acorn's halter. "I'm putting Acorn in the paddock," she said. "Then I'll get Winston to stand up."

"Anna, let Winston die in peace," said Pam.

"He's not dying," shouted Anna. She pulled on Acorn's lead rope. "Come on, Acorn," she said. "I'm putting you outside."

Acorn pulled against Anna. He didn't want to leave the stall.

"Anna," said Pam, "Acorn doesn't want to go outside. He wants to stay here with Winston."

Winston took a deep, noisy breath and closed his eyes.

"Don't you want to say good-bye to Winston, too?" asked Lulu.

Anna looked at Winston through the bars of Acorn's stall. He lay in a heap. Anna tried to imagine him standing up. Or eating hay. Or running around the paddock. Or pulling the driving cart. But she couldn't picture Winston doing any of the things he used to do. And she finally understood that Acorn, Lulu, and Pam were right. Winston was dying.

Anna took off Acorn's halter. She put her face against his cheek. "I'm sorry I yelled at you," she said. Then she went into Winston's stall.

Lulu was gently brushing his mane with her fingers. "Good-bye Winston," she said.

Pam stroked Winston's neck. "You're a wonderful pony, Winston. Ms. Wiggins loves you very much," she told him.

Anna sat beside her friends. She felt tears coming down her cheek. "I don't want him to die," she whispered.

"I know," said Lulu. "Me either."

"I think it's almost the end," said Pam.

"I'll go find Mr. Silver," said Lulu softly. She stood up and left the stall.

Anna leaned over and whispered into Winston's ear, "Ms. Wiggins says good-bye. Good-bye, wonderful Winston. I'll miss you."

A choking sound came from Winston's throat.

Anna remembered that Ms. Wiggins said she wanted Winston to have a peaceful end. And she remembered what Dr. Crandal said about giving Winston an injection to help him die. "Call your father, Pam," said Anna. "We don't want Winston to suffer."

"Okay," said Pam.

Winston's whole body started shaking. Anna had never seen an animal shiver like that. She felt frightened for the old pony. Suddenly, the shivering stopped and Winston's body went limp.

Acorn whinnied a low, sad sound.

Mr. Silver and Lulu rushed into the stall. Mr. Silver squatted beside Winston. He put his head on Winston's barrel-side and listened. Then he put his hand in front of Winston's nose to feel if there was any breath going in and out. Finally, he said, "It was a peaceful end, wasn't it?"

"Yes," said Anna, "very peaceful."

"Just the way Ms. Wiggins wanted it to be," Mr. Silver said.

"I'll call my father," said Pam.

"And tell Mrs. Silver, please." Mr. Silver said. "She was very fond of this pony. We all were." Anna saw tears in Mr. Silver's eyes.

"I'll go with you," Lulu told Pam.

"You coming, Anna?" Pam asked. Anna shook her head.

Pam and Lulu left the barn.

Anna touched Winston's mane one last time. Then she helped Mr. Silver cover Winston's body with a blanket.

Anna went into Acorn's stall. She put her arms around her own pony's neck and cried.

Too Late

Anna put on Acorn's halter and lead rope. He followed her out of the stall.

Anna led her pony to the paddock. "Acorn, you've been inside for a day and night," said Anna. "That's the most you've been indoors since I got you." When Anna let Acorn free, he threw back his head and galloped across the field.

Lightning and Snow White were grazing in the field. They whinnied hellos to Acorn and joined him in his run.

Anna noticed a car coming up the long

driveway. It went past the house and drove up to the barn. Ms. Wiggins stepped out of the car. Anna called out her name and ran to her.

"I came as fast as I could," Ms. Wiggins said. "Anna, am I too late?"

Anna nodded. "Winston died a little while ago." She pointed to the barn. "He's still in there," she said.

Ms. Wiggins turned and walked into the barn. Anna wondered if she should go with her. Then she thought, If it was Acorn who died, I'd want to be alone with him. Anna decided to stay outside and wait for Ms. Wiggins.

Anna noticed Mrs. Silver, Lulu, and Pam come out the back door of the house. They were walking toward the barn. Anna met them near the paddock.

"Ms. Wiggins is back," Anna said. "She's in the barn."

"We saw the car," Pam said.

"She arrived just a few minutes too late," said Mrs. Silver sadly.

"I'd feel so awful if something happened to my pony and I wasn't there," said Lulu.

"Me, too," said Pam.

Mrs. Silver and the Pony Pals waited for Ms. Wiggins by the barn door. No one talked.

Finally, Ms. Wiggins came out. Her eyes were red from crying. In one hand she had the chart that the Pony Pals made for taking care of Winston. In the other hand she carried a thick braid of Winston's mane.

"Thank you for staying with him, girls," she said. She held up the chart. "What you did for Winston and me was so wonderful. I'll never forget it."

"We wanted to help," said Pam.

"Acorn helped, too," said Anna. "He stayed in the stall next to Winston the whole time."

Ms. Wiggins looked at the three ponies and Picasso in the paddock. "Acorn's a terrific pony," she said.

"He's going to miss Winston," said Anna.

"We all will," said Lulu.

Tears were streaming down Ms. Wiggins'

cheeks. The Pony Pals were crying, too. Mrs. Silver put her arm around Ms. Wiggins' shoulder. "Come have some tea, dear," she said. "And maybe a little something to eat."

Ms. Wiggins looked around at the Pony Pals. "Will you come, too?" she asked. "Please."

They nodded that they would.

"Anna didn't have breakfast yet," said Lulu.

Ms. Wiggins smiled at Anna. "Neither did I. Maybe we can convince Mrs. Silver to make us blueberry pancakes."

"The batter is already made," said Mrs. Silver.

Mrs. Silver made pancakes for everyone. And even though Anna felt sad, she was glad to be eating. While they ate, Ms. Wiggins told them stories about Winston. Anna particularly liked the stories from when Ms. Wiggins was her age.

"Once, when I was out alone with him," she said, "I got off to look at a beaver dam.

I accidentally stepped in a hole and twisted my ankle very badly. I couldn't walk. And I couldn't mount Winston again. It was winter and very cold. I was quite frightened. I found a long stick lying near me. I used it to tap Winston and told him to go home. He trotted off. My parents found him on the front lawn. When they saw he was saddled up and alone, they knew something bad had happened. Winston led them to me."

"Winston was a hero," said Pam.

"And a best friend," said Ms. Wiggins.

After breakfast, Ms. Wiggins took out a photo album with pictures of her and Winston. In some pictures Ms. Wiggins was a kid riding Winston. In others, she was a grown-up driving him in a cart. Several of the photos were from the Wiggins Winter Festival parade. Ms. Wiggins and Winston looked happy and proud in those pictures.

Ms. Wiggins closed the photo album. Anna knew that she was feeling tired and sad. "We'd better go," Anna said.

"Thank you for staying with me," Ms. Wiggins said. "And for taking care of Winston."

The Pony Pals didn't talk while they saddled up their ponies. And they were quiet as they rode the Wiggins trails toward Pony Pal Trail. They halted their ponies at the three birches.

"I feel awful for Ms. Wiggins," said Anna.

"I wish we could do something for her," said Lulu.

"We're on vacation, so we have plenty of time to do something really special," said Pam.

"Let's each come up with an idea," said Lulu.

The Pony Pals agreed to meet at Off-Main Diner the next morning to share their ideas.

Anna and Lulu turned their ponies toward home. Anna galloped along Pony Pal Trail. What could the Pony Pals do that would make Ms. Wiggins feel better?

At the Diner

The next morning Anna and Lulu walked over to Off-Main Diner. They saw Lightning tied to the hitching post out front. Lulu and Anna gave Lightning some hello pats and went inside. Pam was already sitting in the Pony Pals' favorite booth. A folded piece of notepaper was on the table in front of her. "Let's share our ideas before we eat anything," said Pam.

Anna was holding a rolled-up piece of drawing paper. Lulu took a small notebook from her jacket pocket.

"You go first, Lulu," said Pam.
Lulu read:

Make a donation to saint Francis
Animal Shelter in memory of Winston.

"That's a great idea," said Pam.

"But I don't have any money," said Anna.
"I spent all my allowance on supplies for Acorn."

"I thought maybe we could collect money from people at the Winter Festival," said Lulu.

"Everyone in town knows Winston from all the years he was in the parade," said Pam. "They'll want to give money."

"I'll decorate a shoe box with drawings of Winston," said Anna. "People can put their donations in that."

"Good idea, Anna," said Lulu.

"What's your idea, Pam?" asked Anna.

Pam read her idea out loud.

Make a sign for Winston.

"We could carry it in the parade," Pam explained.

"I love that idea," said Lulu.

"My idea is about the parade, too," said Anna.

She unrolled her drawing paper and laid it out in the middle of the table.

"My idea is that Ms. Wiggins can drive Acorn in the parade," Anna said. "She wanted Acorn to take Winston's place. I think it would make her feel better if Acorn could do it this year."

"Acorn's only pulled a cart a few times," said Pam. "And the parade is the day after tomorrow."

"Acorn's really smart," said Lulu. "I bet he could do it." She smiled at Anna. "And you learned a lot about driving from Ms. Wiggins. You can train Acorn. We'll help you."

"I don't know," said Pam. "Teaching a pony to drive is a big job."

"We could put the sign about Winston on the back of the driving cart," said Lulu.

"We don't even *have* a driving cart," said Pam.

"But Ms. Wiggins lent me the equipment for ground driving," said Anna. "Let's work with Acorn first. Then we can figure out how to get a cart."

"We have to begin somewhere," said Lulu. "Let's go."

"I guess it's worth a try," said Pam.

Anna went behind the counter and packed up apple juice and doughnuts to go. Her mother came out from the kitchen with a bunch of carrots for the ponies. The Pony Pals didn't tell Mrs. Harley that they were

333

going to train Acorn for the parade. They wanted to surprise everyone.

As soon as they were back at the Harley paddock, the girls started working with Acorn. Anna put on the harness and bridle with blinders. Then she stood behind him holding the long lines. Lulu and Pam stood nearby to help.

"Walk on," Anna called to Acorn. He stood still. His ears went back. Anna told him to walk on again. This time she flicked the lash of the whip against his side. Acorn still didn't move.

"Maybe he's forgotten everything he learned," said Pam.

"Maybe he's being stubborn," said Anna. "Pam, go to his head and give him a pull."

Pam pulled on the lead rope and Acorn walked forward. But when Anna told him to halt he backed up.

Lulu and Pam came over to Anna. "He doesn't obey you when you're ground driving him," Pam said. "It's not safe to hitch him to a cart. Even if we had one."

"There has to be a way we can train Acorn in time to be in the parade," said Lulu. "We can't give up."

"Then we need help," said Pam. "We need a good driving teacher."

"What about your mother, Pam?" asked Anna. "She knows how to drive."

"My mom's going to a special workshop for riding teachers this week," said Pam. "Besides, our driving cart is broken."

"Maybe we should ask Ms. Wiggins to teach Acorn," said Lulu.

"She's too sad to do it," said Anna.

"Besides, we want to surprise her," said Pam.

"Who else could help us?" asked Anna.

"It has to be someone who's an excellent driving teacher," said Lulu.

"And has the equipment," said Pam.

"And who will do it for free," added Anna.

Anna thought hard. Who did they know who could teach Acorn?

A Challenge for Acorn

Lulu and Pam watched Anna take the driving equipment off Acorn. They were all thinking about who could train Acorn in carriage driving.

"I've got it!" shouted Anna. "Mr. Olson!"

"He knows a lot about horses and driving," said Pam.

"And Mr. Olson is a good friend of Ms. Wiggins, too," said Lulu. "I'll bet he'd do it for her."

"Let's go ask him," said Anna.

The girls tacked up their ponies. They

rode east on Main Street to Belgo Road. They took Belgo Road past the diner. Then they made a left onto a dirt trail that went through the woods.

The trail that led to Mr. Olson's farm was one of Anna's favorite rides. But that day she didn't enjoy it. She was worried that Mr. Olson wouldn't be on his horse farm. Or that he wouldn't have time to train Acorn. Or that he'd say Acorn couldn't learn in time for the parade.

"There's Mr. Olson!" shouted Lulu. She pointed to the riding ring. The Pony Pals rode up to Mr. Olson.

"Hello there," called Mr. Olson. He came out of the ring to meet them.

"Ms. Wiggins' pony died," said Anna.

"I heard," he said. "Poor Ms. Wiggins. She loved that pony. Winston was the best driving pony around these parts." Anna thought she saw tears in Mr. Olson's eyes. "We'll miss him in the parade this year."

"That's what we came to talk to you about," said Pam.

338

"Ms. Wiggins was teaching Anna and Acorn driving," said Lulu, "so Acorn could take Winston's place in the parade someday."

"We want to surprise her by putting Acorn in the parade *this* year," said Anna.

"But Acorn's not that good, yet," said Pam. "Will you give him some lessons?"

Mr. Olson rubbed Acorn's muzzle. "How many times has he been hitched up to the cart?" he asked Anna.

"Just a few," said Anna. "But he was pretty good at it."

"And you think he'd be ready to lead a parade in two days?" Mr. Olson asked.

"Acorn's a smart pony," she said.

Mr. Olson didn't say anything for a minute. He looked Acorn in the eye and thought for a minute. Finally he said, "Get that saddle off him, Anna, and let's see what he can do." He looked over at Lulu and Pam. "You two are going to have to help," he said. "And it's not going to be all fun."

"We know," said Lulu as she slid off Snow White.

"We're doing it for Ms. Wiggins," said Pam. She dismounted Lightning.

Mr. Olson pointed to a paddock near the barn. "Put Lightning and Snow White in there," he said. "Then meet me in the barn. You can help bring out the cart and harness. Anna, unsaddle Acorn and wait for me in the ring. We'll start our work there."

First, Mr. Olson ground drove Acorn. Acorn was better behaved for him than he was for Anna. But he still stopped sometimes without being told. "He knows what to do," said Mr. Olson. "He's just being stubborn."

"I know," said Anna.

Mr. Olson hitched Acorn to the cart. He and Anna climbed into the seat. Lulu and Pam stood near Acorn's head and encouraged him to behave. But Acorn wasn't behaving very well.

The three girls and Mr. Olson worked

with Acorn all afternoon. It was a windy winter's day. Anna had on gloves and thick socks, but her hands and feet were still cold. And she knew Pam and Lulu were cold and tired from running around the ring next to Acorn. Once, Lulu slipped in the icy mud. Everyone was working hard and no one complained.

At three o'clock Mr. Olson said, "Enough for today." He shook his head. Anna knew he was discouraged about Acorn. "He could be a terrific little driving pony," Mr. Olson said. "But I doubt we can have him ready for the parade."

"Can we try?" asked Anna. "Please."

"For Ms. Wiggins' sake," added Lulu.

"I'll leave it up to you girls," Mr. Olson said. "If you come by tomorrow, I'll do my part. But I'm warning you, it doesn't look like he'll be good enough for the parade this year."

The Pony Pals rode slowly along the trail. They were cold and tired.

"Let's stop at the diner for some hot chocolate," Anna suggested.

"And talk about what to do," added Lulu.

They tied their ponies to the hitching post in front of the diner and went in. Mrs. Harley made the Pony Pals hot chocolate and grilled cheese sandwiches. They took them in the back to their favorite booth.

The Pony Pals ate and drank silently for a while. Then Pam said, "I don't think Acorn will be ready in time for the parade. Mr. Olson doesn't either."

"Vacation is almost over," said Lulu. "We haven't done half the things we planned."

"Like exploring over near Mt. Morris," said Pam.

Anna listened to her friends. Maybe they were right. Maybe Acorn couldn't learn to be a good driving pony so fast. Maybe she was asking too much of her friends. Maybe she was asking too much of Acorn.

Balloons and Music

"Hello, girls."

Anna looked up.

Ms. Wiggins was walking toward the booth. "I saw three very cute ponies in front of the diner," she said. "So I came in to say hello."

Ms. Wiggins didn't look as tired as she did the day before. But she still looked sad. "Thank you again for everything you did for Winston and me," she said.

"You're welcome," the Pony Pals said.

Ms. Wiggins noticed the poster on the

wall near the booth. It was for the Winter Festival. "Winston just missed being in the parade," she said. "I wish I'd started teaching Acorn driving earlier. Now we'll have to wait until next year, Anna."

Mrs. Harley came over and gave Ms. Wiggins a hug. "Sorry about your pony," she said. "Come have a cup of coffee with me." The two women went to the counter.

When they were gone, the Pony Pals leaned forward to whisper to one another.

"She'd be so glad if Acorn was in the parade," said Lulu.

"We have to try," said Pam. "We'll work all day tomorrow. No matter how cold it is."

"We won't give up," said Anna.

Then Anna had a terrible thought. She told it to her friends. "What if Acorn is in the parade, but Ms. Wiggins isn't there to see him?"

"Look, Ms. Wiggins is leaving," said Lulu.

"We have to make sure she's coming to the parade," said Anna. "Let's go."

The girls rushed out of the diner. Ms. Wiggins was heading toward her car.

" 'Bye, Ms. Wiggins," Lulu said.

" 'Bye, girls," Ms. Wiggins said over her shoulder.

"See you at the parade," added Anna.

Ms. Wiggins stopped and turned to them. "I've decided not to go to the parade this year," she said.

The Pony Pals looked at one another. They had to think of something fast.

"But we're doing something special at the parade," said Pam. "It's in memory of Winston."

"It would be nice if you were there," added Lulu.

Anna was afraid Pam and Lulu were going to give away the surprise by telling Ms. Wiggins that they were training Acorn to be in the parade.

"What are you doing for Winston?" asked Ms. Wiggins.

Anna tried to signal Pam not to say their

plan. Pam winked at Anna and told Ms. Wiggins, "We're going to raise money in memory of Winston."

"And donate it to St. Francis Animal Shelter," added Lulu.

Anna smiled at her friends.

"It would be great if you were at the parade," Anna told Ms. Wiggins.

"What a sweet thing for you girls to do," said Ms. Wiggins. She looked at each of the girls. "A donation to the shelter is a wonderful way to remember Winston. I will see you at the parade."

Ms. Wiggins left and the Pony Pals went to their ponies at the hitching post. "So she wasn't coming to the parade," said Lulu.

"But now she is," said Pam.

"And we only told her one of our three surprises," said Anna. "That was so smart, Pam."

"It was the only thing I could think of," said Pam.

Anna patted Acorn on the neck. "Now all

we have to do is turn Acorn into a terrific driving pony," she said.

The next morning the Pony Pals were at Mr. Olson's farm by nine o'clock. It was a sunny winter day. Everyone was rested and ready for a day of hard work.

The first few times around the ring, Acorn acted as stubborn as the day before. But Mr. Olson knew how to make Acorn pay attention to him. Anna loved riding in the cart, especially when Mr. Olson turned the lines and whip over to her.

"Now we'll go on the driving trail that cuts through the fields," Mr. Olson said. Pam opened the gate. When Acorn was out of the fenced-in ring, he broke into a trot. Mr. Olson scolded and pulled hard on the lines. Acorn halted. Mr. Olson shook his head. Anna knew he was wondering if Acorn could possibly be ready for the parade. But Mr. Olson didn't give up. He kept on working with Acorn and Anna.

After lunch, Mr. Olson handed Lulu a bunch of balloons and a pile of sticks. "You girls blow up these balloons and tie them to the sticks," he said. He pulled two noisemakers out of his jacket pocket. "You'll need these, too."

"Are we having a party?" Anna asked.

"Sort of," said Mr. Olson. "Pam and Lulu are going to wave the balloons, shout, and use the noisemakers near Acorn while he's pulling the cart. He has to be used to the noises of the parade."

"What about music?" asked Anna. "There'll be bands at the parade."

"Good thinking," Mr. Olson said. "There's a radio in the tack room."

The next time Mr. Olson and Anna drove Acorn over the trails, Pam and Lulu ran beside the pony waving the balloons and making noise. Loud music blared from the radio.

Acorn was a little confused at first. He couldn't see where the noise was coming

from because of the blinders. By the third time over the trails, Acorn was used to the noise.

When the lesson was over, they were all tired. Pam and Lulu were hoarse from shouting.

"Is Acorn good enough to be in the parade?" Anna asked Mr. Olson.

"I'm not sure," Mr. Olson said. "I won't know until tomorrow morning. I'll bring the cart to your place early. We can try driving Acorn on the parade route while they're setting up. It'll be a test. If we can drive him on Main Street without any problems, he can be in the parade."

Anna knew that Acorn wasn't a terrific driving pony yet. But Mr. Olson was giving him a chance. Was there anything the Pony Pals could do to help Acorn pass Mr. Olson's driving test?

The Winter Festival

The next morning, the Pony Pals met in Anna's kitchen. She showed them the box she had made for contributions in memory of Winston.

"We'll pass around the donation box, Anna," said Lulu "You'll be busy driving Acorn with Mr. Olson."

"I don't know if Acorn can do it," Anna said. "He wasn't very good yesterday."

"Mr. Olson said if he isn't perfect this morning, he can't be in the parade," said Pam.

"Why isn't he being a good driving pony?" asked Lulu. "Ms. Wiggins said he'd be good."

"I think he misses Winston," said Lulu.

"I wish Winston was here to drive in front of him," said Pam. "Then I bet Acorn would be fine."

"Acorn loves to be with his pony friends," said Lulu.

Anna had an idea. "That's it!" she shouted. "I know what we can do so Acorn will drive better." She jumped up. "Hurry. Let's go to the paddock. We have to be ready when Mr. Olson gets here."

"Ready for what?" asked Pam.

As they ran to the paddock, Anna told them her plan.

When Mr. Olson's pickup pulled into the driveway with the cart, the Pony Pals were ready. "Bring Acorn here," he told Anna. "Well hook him up to the cart in the driveway."

Anna led Acorn out of the paddock and up the driveway. Pam and Lulu followed, riding Lightning and Snow White. Mr. Olson was surprised to see them on their ponies. "I thought you two were going to help us with the driving," he said.

"We are helping," said Lulu.

"We're going to ride in front of Acorn," said Pam.

"If Acorn's friends are walking in front of him, he'll work better," said Anna. "I just know it."

Mr. Olson smiled. "The Pony Pals are always coming up with powerful ideas," he said. "It's worth a try."

Main Street was closed to traffic. People were preparing for the Winter Festival. A tent and booths were being put up on the Town Green. Mr. Harley was starting a fire in the volunteer firemen's huge barbecue pit. And the band was warming up.

Anna knew that the activity wouldn't bother Snow White and Lightning. And it wouldn't bother Acorn, if she were riding him. But today Acorn was pulling a cart and wearing blinders.

Anna and Mr. Olson climbed into the cart.

Pam and Lulu took the lead down Main Street. Anna held her breath. Mr. Olson signaled Acorn to follow. Acorn walked behind his pony friends and kept a good pace. Suddenly a policeman ran into the road. He blew a whistle and signaled the Pony Pal parade to stop. A group of Boy Scouts, shouting and laughing, ran across the road in front of them. Snow White and Lightning stood quietly. So did Acorn.

Mr. Olson turned to Anna and smiled. "I have a feeling Acorn will pass this test," he said.

Half an hour later, the Pony Pals were in the school parking lot ready to lead off the parade. Anna's older sister, Melissa, came up to them. She said that hundreds of people were standing along School Street and Main Street to watch the parade. She held up the contribution box. "I have to empty it," Melissa said. "It's stuffed to the top, and more people want to contribute! They all loved Winston."

"Good work," said Pam.

"Where's Ms. Wiggins?" asked Anna.

"In front of Town Hall," Melissa said.

The band struck up a marching song. The festival organizer signaled to Pam and Lulu to start the parade. They directed their ponies onto School Street. Mr. Olson told Acorn to walk on and he did.

Acorn held his head high, his ears were forward, and he walked with a beautiful stride. The cart seemed to glide behind him. People cheered. Anna turned to her right and left and smiled at her neighbors.

Anna saw Ms. Wiggins in front of Town Hall with Melissa. Ms. Wiggins was surprised to see Lightning and Snow White in the parade. Then she saw Acorn pulling the cart. She waved and smiled to Anna. Anna waved back. When Lulu and Pam reached Town Hall, they stopped their ponies. Mr. Olson halted Acorn. Anna motioned for Ms. Wiggins to come over.

"Want to climb aboard?" Mr. Olson asked Ms. Wiggins. She nodded. Mr. Olson told Melissa to hold Acorn by the bridle. Then he handed the reins and whip to Anna and stepped out of the cart. Ms. Wiggins climbed in next to Anna. The band began a new song. The festival organizer signaled Lulu and Pam to ride on. Anna held the lines out for Ms. Wiggins, but she shook her head no. "You drive, Anna," she said. "It's your turn. Yours and Acorn's."

Anna and Ms. Wiggins were smiling. But they both had tears in their eyes.

The parade went around the Town

Green, up School Street, and ended in the parking lot. Anna and Ms. Wiggins climbed out of the cart. There was still one surprise that Ms. Wiggins didn't know about.

"Look at the back of the cart," Anna told Ms. Wiggins. Anna held Acorn by the bridle while Ms. Wiggins walked behind the cart. She read the sign aloud.

Winston. 30 Years.
Goodbye to a Wonderful Pony.

A crowd gathered around the pony and cart. "Is this pony taking Winston's place in the parade?" someone asked.

"Yes, he is," said Ms. Wiggins.

"What's his name?" another person asked.

"His name is Acorn," answered Anna. She put her hand on Acorn's mane. "Winston and Acorn were friends."

"Hooray for Acorn!" someone shouted.

People clapped. Anna gave Acorn a great big hug. "You did it, Acorn," she told him. "You did it."